PRESUMED DEAD

NICHOLE SEVERN

D0054575

H HARLEQUIN

INTRIGUE

For the Harlequin Intrigue authors: you inspire me on a daily basis. Keep writing.

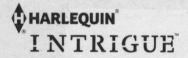

Recycling programs
for this product may
not exist in your area.

ISBN-13: 978-1-335-58304-8

Presumed Dead

Copyright © 2022 by Natascha Jaffa

For questions and comments about the quality of this book, please contact us at CustomerService@Harlequin.com.

Harlequin Enterprises ULC
22 Adelaide St. West, 41st Floor
Toronto, Ontario M5H 4E3, Canada
www.Harlequin.com

Printed in U.S.A.

She had to be careful around him. One mistake was all it would take to destroy her future.

The seconds ticked by in silence. Campbell didn't know what to say, what to think. Her brain tried to convince her the man sitting across from her was nothing but a stranger, but her heart knew better. "It's nice to see the locals still come here after everything that happened."

"Is that why you showed up in the middle of my investigation? To talk about a diner that's seen better days?" Kendric took a slow pull of his coffee, the steam twisting and arching over scars that demanded attention.

"Would you rather talk about how I came off shift one night to find your side of the bed empty, your half of the closet cleaned out and a note that said, 'I'm sorry'?" She hadn't meant to let the past infiltrate the present but hiding the anger didn't mean it hadn't gone away. It'd just gotten more volatile.

"What do you want me to say, Campbell? We both know why I left."

The hell she did.

Nichole Severn writes explosive romantic suspense with strong heroines, heroes who dare challenge them and a hell of a lot of guns. She resides with her very supportive and patient husband, as well as her demon spawn, in Utah. When she's not writing, she's constantly injuring herself running, rock climbing, practicing yoga and snowboarding. She loves hearing from readers through her website, www.nicholesevern.com, and on Facebook, @nicholesevern.

Books by Nichole Severn

Harlequin Intrigue

Defenders of Battle Mountain

Grave Danger
Dead Giveaway
Dead on Arrival
Presumed Dead

A Marshal Law Novel

The Fugitive
The Witness
The Prosecutor
The Suspect

Blackhawk Security

Rules in Blackmail
Rules in Rescue
Rules in Deceit
Rules in Defiance
Caught in the Crossfire
The Line of Duty

Visit the Author Profile page at Harlequin.com.

CAST OF CHARACTERS

Kendric Hudson—Battle Mountain's newest reserve officer has worked crime scenes before, but his gut is telling him the abduction of an expectant mother isn't as it seems.

Campbell Dwyer—She's assigned to assist BMPD for one reason: to find the truth. But her work for the state's Internal Affairs Unit has her wondering if the department isn't involved in the largest crime spike in years. Can Kendric trust her to back him up and bring a missing woman home?

Sabrina Bryon—The expectant mother has been taken in the dead of night, leaving an injured husband and pool of blood behind. But the questions don't stop there.

Cree Gregson—Kendric's best friend and former Larimer County bomb squad tech, now reserve officer for Battle Mountain.

Weston Ford—Battle Mountain's police chief's only concern is keeping his town safe...no matter the cost.

Chapter One

Battle Mountain had lost its innocence.

Because of him.

Reserve Officer Kendric Hudson climbed the built-in ramp leading up to the cabin's front door. Trees of every size and age—along with the surrounding snow-covered mountains—seemed to suffocate the bare acreage around them. Wouldn't have taken much for the kidnapper to get in and out without being seen.

No one would've even heard Sabrina Bryon scream.

He scanned the small living room for signs of a struggle, coming up empty. There wasn't much to the place. Dated. Neglected. Just like the rest of the town. A simple kitchen with the brightest blue countertops he'd ever seen stood off to the right, an old-school woodburning stove, the kind pioneers would've used a hundred years ago, to the left. According to the 911 call from the husband, the abduction had taken place in the early morning hours. The victim would've been in bed, asleep.

His boots reverberated off worn hardwood as he slipped a pair of latex gloves over his hands. Despite the majestic views, bone-chilling silence and the fact he could escape on a property like this for hours, he was standing in the middle of a crime scene. He couldn't make any mistakes.

Rounding into the back half of the house, Kendric took in the first bedroom decorated in pink wallpaper, a fuzzy rug and a glittery mobile hanging above an empty crib. Sunlight pierced through the open blinds, and his gut twisted harder than he'd expected. He kept moving. This wasn't his first rodeo, but he never could get comfortable with crimes involving kids. Not like the agents he'd worked with in the ATF. Detached. Single-minded. Job oriented. To them, it wasn't about the victims affected by the psychopaths they set out to dismantle. It was about solving the case, about reassembling the crime and catching the culprit. For a while, he'd convinced himself he'd been one of them.

Then Battle Mountain had gone up in flames.

A place he'd never been before in his life, one he hadn't intended on getting to know.

Now he'd do whatever it took to make up for the pain the people of this sleepy old mining town had suffered.

"Gregson." He moved into the controlled chaos of the master bedroom, targeting the former Larimer County bomb expert turned reserve officer. A flash popped from the camera in Gregson's hands. As Battle Mountain's few protectors, the officers here had a responsibility to cover every base. Evidence collection, scene photography, witness statements, securing perimeters and the thousand other tasks required to uncover the truth. Without federal or state resources. That lack of support was what had driven Kendric to leave everything—and everyone—he'd known behind and start something new. It was the least he could do after Battle Mountain's entire Main Street had been under the siege of a bomber. "Any word from the kidnapper?"

A stretch of fresh burn scars added to the intelligence and experience in Cree Gregson's expression, the very air around the town's newest officer thick with control. His own scars tingled with remembered pain as he took in the scene through his dominant eye. The one not impacted by scar tissue hanging from his eyebrow. For the two of them, fire had changed their lives in a single event. And nearly taken them. If Gregson hadn't pulled that hero crap on an assignment gone bad that had left the former tech with a stretch of mangled skin down his back, Kendric wouldn't be here at all.

"Not yet." Gregson maneuvered around the end of the queen-size bed. "Alma's with the husband at the hospital. He's touch and go. Nothing he's saying is making sense right now. The EMTs had to sedate him. They're not sure he's going to make it. From what I can tell, perp walked right in the front door, came straight back here to the bedrooms. Husband wakes up, tries to fight back here in the hallway. The struggle moves into the bedroom. Kidnapper puts two rounds into him for making trouble, leaving a pool of blood on this side of the bed and takes our vic. Sabrina Bryon. Twenty-eight-year-old female. Married to Elliot Bryon, going on two years."

"The kidnapper knew the layout of the house. He's done his homework, got access." Or he'd been in the house before. But why not make the ransom demand? Why go through all the trouble—and an attempted murder charge—without getting something out of this in the end? Kendric hiked a thumb over his shoulder. "And the baby? I passed a nursery on the way in."

"Sabrina Bryon's pregnant. About eight

months, according to the ultrasound taped on the fridge," Gregson said. "A girl."

Damn. "You're thinking this is a two-for-one deal. Take mother and child, ransom them both, but put in half the work. Is the husband talking?"

"Not with a bullet in his chest," an all-too-familiar voice said from behind. "His lung was on the verge of collapse in the ambulance on the way to Grand Junction. Unfortunately for us, Elliot Bryon won't be saying anything for a while."

Ice clawed through Kendric's veins. He turned to face the blonde investigator capable of castrating a man with a single glare of those cerulean blue eyes. The form-fitting pantsuit did nothing to hide a lean, feminine frame Kendric had tried to forget. Waves of silk hair cascaded over her shoulders and down her back, and his fingers curled in memory of what they'd felt like in his hands.

Campbell Dwyer scanned the room as though he didn't even exist. Then again, he'd made it perfectly clear when he'd left Loveland, that he couldn't. Not in her life. She'd had her sights on transferring out of her small-time investigative duties for Larimer's sheriff's department, and as a bomb tech barely hanging on to his own skin, he hadn't fit into that plan. He'd done what he'd thought was best. For both of them. "Detective Dwyer. I wasn't aware Colorado's Bureau of Investigations had an interest in small-town abductions. Isn't that a little beneath your pay grade?"

"Isn't playing cop in a town nobody's heard of beneath yours?" She moved into the room, giving him a wide berth, every inch the intense, defensive woman he remembered. Always knew exactly where to strike, too.

His new life with the ATF after surviving a bombing had ended the moment one of his colleagues had tried to burn Battle Mountain to the ground with a series of explosives to cover up a murder. Rescue crews, the town's entire Main Street, and Gregson and his partner, Alma Majors, were all still trying to recover. Kendric studied the exposed skin of Campbell's wrists, her bare fingernails—cut too short—and the elaborate but subtle detail of her makeup. Still the epitome of opposites. Even after all this time.

He forced his attention to Gregson. To prove she didn't still have a hold on him. "I take it the state's powers that be want one of their own involved in this investigation to keep an eye on things. Make sure the small-town folk are doing their jobs right."

"You certainly haven't lost your deduction skills since making your career change, have you?" Armed with a set of her own latex gloves, Campbell extracted an evidence bag from her blazer and crouched. She targeted the broken wristwatch on the floor beside the bed. "May I?"

"I've got everything I need," Gregson said.

"Battle Mountain has seen two spree killers, a serial killer and a rogue ATF agent try to rip this town apart in less than a year. Even you can understand that raises some red flags, Agent…" She squinted, turning toward Kendric, the watch still in hand. "I'm sorry, what are you now?"

His jaw ached under the pressure of his back teeth. She knew very well what he was. Just as he'd followed her career after a bomb had failed to rip off his face, she would've done her homework on him before taking this assignment. "Officer."

"Right. Officer." Her gaze skimmed down the length of his chest, the corners of her mouth softening. "You always were eager to side with the underdogs, Kendric. This place suits you."

"Dwyer." Gregson extended his hand in greeting, and Kendric realized he'd created an alternate universe in which only he and Campbell had existed. "It's been a while."

Right. The crime scene. A missing young mother. A husband in the hospital. And a whole lot of unanswered questions. "You remember Cree Gregson."

"Of course. Good to see there's someone here keeping Kendric out of trouble. I've read your report concerning your last case. Your partner's, too. Impressive work. The both of you." The undertone in Campbell's voice conveyed her confusion over why his friend had given up a promising career in explosive ordinance to play cop in a town this small. Like Kendric had. Her eyes tracked to his, and her point drove home.

Suspicion lodged in his gut. As much as he hated to admit he'd missed their own personal brand of banter, it wouldn't change the fact she wasn't supposed to be here. "Cut to the chase, Campbell. What does CBI want with a simple abduction case? Our department is more than capable of running point for Sabrina Bryon's safe return. Unless you were invited by Chief Ford himself, you don't have jurisdiction here."

"Actually, I do." Campbell lowered the wristwatch she'd collected from the floor into an evidence bag, then pulled a folded piece of paper from the inside of her blazer. She handed it off, and every cell in his body burned in warning. "Take a look for yourself."

Gregson stepped behind him to look at the directive over his shoulder. Kendric read through the brief signed by none other than the CBI director himself. What the hell? "This says—"

"That's right." She sealed the evidence bag. "It says this case falls under the jurisdiction of the Colorado Bureau of Investigation in the name of public safety, and that through a series of fortunate events, they sent their lead missing persons case agent to take point and negotiate the ransom for Sabrina Bryon on their behalf. In case you're having a hard time processing that little tidbit, that would be me."

How was this possible? Campbell didn't have this kind of pull on her own. She would've had to convince someone high up to put her here. What kind of favors had she called in to get herself assigned to his case and why?

The low *thunk* of her heels ticked off in rhythm to the headache pulsing at the base of his skull. Handing over the watch to Kendric, Campbell penetrated his personal space. "Look on the bright side, Kendric. Looks like you and I get to be partners again."

HER HANDS SHOOK as she peeled her gloves free and stepped outside.

Campbell Dwyer had been waiting for this

moment. Rehearsed conversations, practiced reactions under the stress of seeing him again. Detachment. None of it had worked. At least not for her. Kendric, on the other hand… He'd barely registered any kind of emotion when she'd stepped into the room. How was that for closure after all these years?

She walked the perimeter of the small cabin surrounded by walls of intimidating nature. Kendric had been a city boy through and through. What could've possibly urged him to leave his life, his extended family, his friends and his career to relocate to the middle of nowhere? Dirt skimmed over the toes of her heels as she studied the scene.

Sabrina Bryon, twenty-eight years old, married to Elliot Bryon a little less than six years. No living relatives. No record of domestic disputes. Good credit history. Nothing to suggest she was in financial or physical danger. The victim worked as an online English teacher. Not the kind of profession targeted for a large payday, but the Bryons weren't clawing out of poverty, either. The calendar pinned near the front door of the cabin had listed two recent appointments. Both for the ob-gyn Campbell intended to interview as soon as she was done here. Her heart squeezed behind her rib cage until her lungs spasmed for another breath of air. Battle Mountain had become a hunting ground for the worst kinds of criminals, and their missing victim had just been the latest in a long line of reasons why she'd been assigned to take a look. But without contact from the kidnappers, they had nothing to propel this case forward.

"How did you get to the house without waking them up?" Campbell mused out loud.

If Sabrina's abductor had used the main road, there should've been tire tracks, something to tell them how the UNSUB—the unknown subject—had arrived and escaped. Rounding to the front of the cabin, she targeted a deep set of impressions that matched others in the dirt driveway. The victim's car? If the abductor had taken it to escape with his target, where was the vehicle he'd arrived in?

At the back of the structure, Campbell caught sight of a series of boot prints. One set in. One set out. She unpocketed her phone and took a photo of the design. Size ten, maybe eleven. Ridged, like a hiking boot. Patches of grass made it difficult to ascertain whether anyone else had come this way. Whoever had surprised the Bryons had been prepared for the terrain. "You had to be strong enough to carry Sabrina out on your own."

In her experience, women tended to gain between twenty to fifty pounds during pregnancy. It wouldn't have been easy to manage on his own. Unless the victim hadn't fought back.

"Talking to yourself again?" Kendric's deep tone resonated through her. It triggered a chain reaction starting with a gut clench and ending with heat flaring up her neck. No matter how many times she'd tried to protect herself against his effects, he'd always had the effortless ability to let her know she could wind up as his next meal.

And she'd liked being his chew toy while it had lasted.

"The voices in my head get cranky if I don't answer." Straightening, Campbell turned to face him. The air between them seemed to shift with tension and resentment, and tightened the muscles down her spine. His intelligent, piercing green eyes intensified her discomfort in stepping into his investigation, but from where she was standing, neither of them really had a choice. They'd been trained to follow orders. Even in his new position as one of this town's first line of defense, that hadn't changed. "That was a joke."

"I see you haven't lost your terrible sense of humor." Kendric leaned against the side of the house, arms crossed over a broad chest. Styled, dark hair matched the thin beard growth he'd let get out of hand. There was a reason for it, a self-consciousness he obviously still couldn't escape, but the scars that had contorted the skin along one side of his face had never bothered her. He'd just used them as an excuse to push everyone away.

"You used to laugh at my cheesy jokes." She'd tried so hard to let go of the past, to banish it, but it was always there just under the surface. Waiting to stab her in the heart all over again. "I've got a set of boot prints. One set in and out, heading for those trees over there. I haven't followed them yet, but they look to belong to the same UNSUB. Are you equipped to take impressions?"

"We're not as backward out here as you might think, Detective. I'll get the kit from my vehicle." He disappeared around the same corner where he'd ambushed her.

Detective. The title grated against her nerves. If he was going through anything like she was at seeing him again, he'd hidden it behind a very thick layer of rock-hard annoyance. Or maybe her hopes of finding him as miserable as she was since their breakup five years ago had been nothing but a fantasy. "Get yourself together, Dwyer."

Footsteps registered from behind, and she realized Kendric was making an effort to announce his arrival this time. He settled the kit into the dirt beside her and popped the lid. Without so much as a glance in her direction, he handed off a photo evidence ruler and pulled an aerosol can of dust and dirt hardener. She positioned the ruler beside the boot print and took another photo right before he handed off the hardener. He mixed the casting material and solution into a small mixing bowl with a spatula and reached over her to pour it into the mold.

They moved as though they'd done this a thousand times. In a way, they had. Dozens of cases she and Kendric had partnered on with the sheriff's department reeled through her mind. Him as a bomb technician. Her as a detective. They'd met and fallen head over heels doing this very kind of work. Evidence collection, crime scene searches, following leads. She wouldn't have been able to close any of them without his ordinance expertise, and he hadn't been able to put the pieces together without her investigative skills.

They'd made one hell of a team.

And created something amazing in the process.

Until the bombing that had nearly killed him.

"I was surprised to hear you'd taken a job

out here as a reserve officer." She watched as each centimeter of casting solution hardened, one section after the other. The longer they took to process the scene, the higher risk they'd lose evidence. They didn't have time to wait for the cast to dry before following the trail into the trees, but she couldn't seem to break this moment, either. Not yet. "Can't imagine what could've pulled you away from the ATF. I thought becoming one of their instructors was what you'd wanted."

"It was." Kendric shifted his weight between both heels, still so unwilling to give up that legendary control. It was aggravating, really. Because the man testing the edges of the footprint cast beside her wasn't the man she'd known at all. "Until one of my colleagues set this town on fire to cover up a murder."

"Agent Freehan." Campbell still couldn't get comfortable with the fact a federal agent had taken her extensive knowledge in explosives and used it against the very people she'd been sworn to protect. "I reviewed the reports on my way down. She used a series of explosions to cover up the murder of her sister, even started a forest fire in the process."

Kendric pried the cast from the footprint. The rubber bent and flexed at his direction but kept its perfect shape of the treads left behind. They'd compare it to the homeowner's shoes to eliminate the potential for error. He secured the cast into an evidence bag from the kit and sealed it inside. "Guess it was only a matter of time."

"What does that mean?" she asked.

"Doesn't matter." Shoving to his feet, he headed toward the trees. "We need to see where these tracks end. The kidnapper might've been strong enough to carry Sabrina Bryon from the house, but he wouldn't last in this wilderness without transportation."

Another layer of distance wedged between them. Right when she thought she'd gotten a hand on his determination to keep her at arm's length, he changed the game. Mud clung to her heels and threatened to suction them off her feet as she followed along the tracks. Their kidnapper had been prepared for this terrain. She wasn't.

Kendric disappeared into the trees, every ounce a predator she hadn't expected. He was comfortable here, aware, knowledgeable. He liked it here, and a sour taste spread over her tongue. He wasn't a small-town cop. He'd investigated terrorist attacks, served his country and saved lives on a large scale. This wasn't him. "Over here."

Her legs and feet cramped as she struggled across the uneven ground. Frost clung to shrubs and bushes and melted against her skin the deeper into the trees she dared. Warning iced through her as sunlight failed to breach through the thick canopy above. Silence crystallized around her. Her breath fogged in front of her mouth. "Kendric?"

No movement. No sign of him ahead. The trail of boot prints had vanished in the undergrowth of foliage, rocks and broken twigs. They'd never be able to search this entire plot of land. Not with the limited amount of resources Battle Mountain PD held. She hunkered into her thin blazer. Her ankles threatened to buckle as the cold sank past her clothing and into muscle and tendons.

A hand latched around her arm.

Campbell reached for her sidearm a split second before recognition flared. Kendric. Her lungs collapsed as she released the breath she'd been holding. "What are you doing? I could've shot you."

"Bet that wasn't even the first time you thought about it." Offering his hand, he helped her cut through a particularly thick bush. Calluses scraped along the inside of her palm as Kendric led her to a fallen tree that had been carved out over decades by insect, wild animal and erosion activity. He nodded at one end and released her hand. "Take a look."

Campbell circled to meet him. And froze. "Is that…?"

Auburn hair splayed over the edges of weathered wood. Leaves wove through the tangled mess and clung to pale skin. Nausea churned in her stomach as she took in crusted blood, torn clothing, waxy discoloration and obvious similarities to their missing woman. Darkness encased the body from the shoulders down. Whoever had stuffed the victim inside hadn't wanted her found. Not until they were ready.

"It's not Sabrina Bryon." Kendric pulled a flashlight from his coat and highlighted the woman staring up at them. Same hair color, similar frame. The resemblance was uncanny to someone who hadn't studied photos of their missing woman all morning. Only this woman wasn't pregnant. "But someone went through a hell of a lot of trouble to make us think she is."

Chapter Two

They didn't have an identification.

The woman he and Campbell had recovered seemed to fit the same basic criteria to describe their missing victim, but he noted distinct differences between them now that the coroner had removed the body from the tree to begin her on-site examination. Her teeth, for one, were far too uneven to match the recent photos taken of Sabrina Bryon. Wrong color, too. According to the town's dentist— Dr. Corsey—the missing mother had taken great care of her teeth and had gone through years of braces and whitening to show for it. This woman had never met an orthodontist in her life.

Then there was the fact she wasn't pregnant.

"Do you have any idea who she is?" Campbell folded her arms across her chest, her expression carefully set. She'd investigated plenty of homicides with the sheriff's department, had learned to remove emotion from the equation to get a better understanding of evidence. Why had he expected this one to be any different?

"No." He watched as Dr. Chloe Pascale pierced through the woman's side with a liver thermometer. He didn't know much about medical exams and autopsies, and he was sure as hell going to keep it that way. "I sent a photo to Chief Ford to see if he or Macie recognized her. They have no idea who she is. He's got his brother Easton and Officer Majors headed to the properties around here to get a possible ID. See if someone recognizes her. Hard to believe she wasn't involved in what went down this morning, given her proximity to the scene."

"She was pretending to be pregnant." She nodded to the round pillow with straps Cree Gregson was pulling from the other end of the tree. "Men sometimes strap them around their stomachs to experience the feeling of pregnancy. Whoever she was, I think you're right. She had to be involved in Sabrina Bryon's abduction."

He couldn't argue. It wasn't a coincidence they'd followed the only set of footprints from the primary scene right where a body had been dumped. Jane Doe hadn't walked herself out here to be stuffed in a tree. But the connection between their victim and the Bryons was still out of reach. "That's an odd piece of trivia to know. You have much experience with pregnancy pillows?"

He regretted the question the moment it escaped his mouth. In reality, he had no right to ask about her life. He'd walked out of it because he hadn't been able to stand the thought of her committing herself to a lost cause. Losing feeling in one side of his face had only been the beginning. He'd just saved her from going down with the ship. "Sorry. None of my business."

"I asked you why you relocated to Battle Mountain. Guess it's only fair for you to ask personal questions, too." Campbell didn't elaborate as she circled around the sanitary sheet the coroner had placed under the body. "That looks like a small-caliber entrance wound in her back. Not a whole lot of blood. Thin smudge ring, little contusion. I'd say from a .22. Do we know what kind of weapon the husband was shot with yet?"

Admiration filtered through his tunneled focus on the victim. As much as he hated to accept Campbell's help in this case, she had a better handle on homicide investigations than he did. Give him a scene in which a bomber had gutted an entire town with a single device planted in the Battle Mountain police station, and he could tell investigators the experience level of the bomber, pull DNA from the components and reassemble the thing blind. This was a whole new ball field in which he was playing an entirely different game. But that still didn't explain why CBI had sent her.

"No word from Grand Junction just yet, but I'll be sure to follow up with them to run a comparison." Dr. Chloe Pascale bagged both of the victim's hands to protect any evidence under the fingernails and preserve prints. With any luck, she'd be able to match dental, DNA or fingerprints to give their victim a name. "From what I can see, the deceased was shot from a distance. The bullet was small enough to pass through the back of the rib cage and nick the right atrium of the heart. There isn't any sign of an exit wound from my preliminary exam, but I'll know more once I get her back to the funeral home."

"The funeral home?" Campbell's gaze cut to him a split second before her laugh died on her lips. "You're joking, right?"

"Thank you, Dr. Pascale. We'll be in touch." Kendric hiked his way through the density of underbrush as Gregson and the coroner searched what was left of their scene. Every second Sabrina Bryon was missing was another second she might not make it home alive. They had to keep moving.

Campbell caught up with him, slightly out of breath, and he couldn't help but enjoy watching her squirm out here in the great outdoors. Out of the two of them, she'd always been the one least acquainted with adapting. "She wasn't joking, was she? Battle Mountain has to perform their autopsies in the back of a funeral home. Do you even have a forensic lab to process evidence?"

He pulled up short, facing her. "What are you really doing here, Campbell? Why did you take this case?"

"You read the letter." Defensiveness ticked the small muscles in her jaw. "Given the drastic rise in crime here, the CBI wants to keep a close eye on this one. I'm the lead missing persons case agent. It made sense for me to be the one assigned."

"That's bullshit, and you know it. You never take a case without doing your homework first. You knew I'd left the ATF after my last investigation for them. You followed me here. Why?" His gut warned him to back down, to let it go, but he'd never been one to follow his instincts. Not when it came to her.

Color drained from her face, her mouth parting slightly. "You've got some nerve. Because from where I'm standing, I'm the one with experience here. Your department is unequipped and undertrained to bring Sabrina Bryon home. What you should be saying, Kendric, is thank you. So let's cut the pleasantries, shall we? My assignment here has nothing to do with you. Despite what your ego might be telling you, I've moved on. And in case you've forgotten, I don't let my personal life compromise my cases." Campbell tucked her hands into her blazer pockets. "Now, are you going to help me bring Sabrina home, or do I need to partner with Gregson on this one? Think about it."

She didn't wait for a response, balancing on those ridiculous heels as she headed back toward the Bryon cabin. Hell, the clock had already started ticking for their victim, and he'd wasted precious time suspecting Campbell had an ulterior motive. She was right. They had a job to do. Even if it meant working with the one person he'd told himself he couldn't ever see again.

"Damn it." He scrubbed a hand down his face, then rushed to keep up with her escape. Following her across the wraparound porch, Kendric blocked her entrance back into the cabin. "Fine. You were right. You're more qualified to recover Sabrina Bryon than I am, but that doesn't mean you're taking the lead. I know this town. I've gotten to know the people here, and the last thing they need is a CBI investigator making their lives harder than they already are. So we do this my way. Understand?"

"Understood." Campbell straightened.

"Good. In that case you should know, yes, Dr. Pascale was serious about doing her examinations in the back of a funeral home. And no, we don't have a forensic lab to analyze trace evidence. Everything we've pulled from the body and this scene will be sent to Unified Forensics in Denver." He didn't know what else she wanted from him, but the urge to settle the dust between them struck hard. "Whatever else you need to find Sabrina Bryon, it's yours."

Tension drained from her shoulders. "I don't think this was a kidnapping for ransom. Elliot Bryon is the only one who would've paid, but the kidnapper took him out of the equation the second he was given the chance."

She was right. Why shoot the only person who could meet the ransom demands? It was Kidnapping 101. "Abduction gone wrong, then?"

"I don't think so." The defensiveness left her expression, leaving behind soft eyes filled with compassion and urgency. "Whoever shot Elliot

Bryon brought the gun for a reason. It's possible getting him and Jane Doe out of the way was the plan all along, in which case our missing vic is in more danger than we believed. Either way, once we identify the woman in those woods, we'll have a better chance of connecting her to who's behind this."

"Then this is strictly about Sabrina Bryon." Admiration sucker punched him in the gut all over again as though he'd been physically hit. The way her mind worked effortlessly to connect the pieces was something he'd never been able to ignore. It was what made her a great investigator. This was what she was good at, what she was trained for. "The kidnapper wanted her for a reason."

"Or her baby." Her gaze snapped to his, and his insides went cold. "Most kidnappings throughout the country fall under parental, and from there a female relative is the most likely suspect. Sometimes they believe the child is in danger and the abduction is out of a sense of protection. Other times it's because of jealousy or financial gain, but this… I don't think a woman is behind this."

"What makes you so sure?" he asked.

She slipped her hands into her slacks. "Women tend to internalize their problems. They don't manifest frustrations or emotional injuries aggressively. Instead, they'll become self-destructive. Drug or alcohol use, suicide attempts, punishing themselves. Very few women actually have the capability of putting two bullets in an innocent man. Add that to the fact Sabrina Bryon was carried out of here, we're likely looking for a male UNSUB."

"Hell, sounds like you don't have much use for me." His laugh took him by surprise.

"Yeah, well, when you've worked as many of these cases as I have, you tend to pick up a few things." Her mouth lost its curl. "And you miss others."

The weight of that statement—combined with the drop in her voice—said it had happened one too many times, and his heart rate ticked up a notch. "I'll have Gregson and Majors start the canvass. Maybe one of the neighbors heard or saw something."

"We should also get in touch with her obgyn. They've most likely drawn blood from both parents throughout Sabrina's pregnancy to run genetic testing." Campbell tugged her phone from her slacks. "They'd be the ones to compare Elliot's DNA to the fetus."

Did all women know this much about pregnancy and babies? "You're thinking the baby might not be his. There was no evidence of another woman in the house or in the vehicle here."

Campbell nodded, her attention scrolling across the porch. "That's the thing about secrets. Three people can keep one, if two of them are dead."

THE CANVASS HADN'T turned up anything solid.

Then again, with more than a few acres between each home out here in the middle of nowhere, she hadn't expected much. Still, no recollections of gunshots. No sounds of screams or a car engine. The only 911 call had come from within the Bryon home itself, after Sabrina had been taken. Apparently gunshots weren't rare in a town that lived for hunting season and the Second Amendment.

Campbell paged through a collection of personnel records between bites of something she could only describe as the best thing she'd ever eaten. Considering she hadn't slowed down long enough for a meal in the past twenty-four hours, that wasn't saying much. Greta's on Main was small but mighty. The scent of smoke still clung to the walls of the original town diner and blackened old mining recruiting signs screwed into the tiled wall. This place had been lucky to escape the bombing that had occurred a few doors down two months ago.

Not many other establishments on Main Street could say the same.

She flipped open the cover of the next file, her heart jumping in her chest at the official photo paper-clipped on the first page. Kendric. Before an explosion disfigured one side of his face. Postured in official dress blues, he stared straight at the camera as though daring her to look away.

He'd always been handsome. Charming, warm. But an ecoterrorist attack during one of Loveland's annual conferences had changed everything. For him, for them. She traced the photo with the edge of her thumb. She hated the hot and cold vibe she'd gotten from him at the scene this morning when she knew what lay under all that resentment and bitterness. He had every right to be angry with the damage he'd sustained from the bombing, but it hadn't stopped him from being the strongest man she'd ever known.

Time and space should've dulled her emotional response to him, but faced with the likelihood of working this abduction case together, she found it only stronger. A reminder of how much power he'd wielded over her from the beginning. She'd compartmentalized the hurt of their breakup, but that obviously wasn't working anymore. She'd missed their connection, his smile, the way he always made her feel safe and protected. Now there was nothing but a hardened shell beneath the scars.

"Wasn't expecting you here." His voice held a hint of detachment as he moved into her peripheral vision, and Campbell closed the file she'd been reading.

Tucking the stack onto the pleather booth beside her, she secured her hands around her near-empty coffee cup as he took a seat across from her. "I didn't realize we were having lunch together today."

"Jane Doe is on her way to the funeral home with the promise Dr. Pascale will call as soon as she has a match to fingerprints, DNA or dental scans. And the forensic evidence we collected is headed to Denver. I also took the liberty of comparing the cast of the footprints outside to the homeowner's shoes. No match." He interlaced his fingers, then splayed them wide as though not sure of how he used to act around her. "Until we get the analysis of the blood and gunpowder from the scene, there's not a whole lot we can do."

The burn of guilt slid up her throat as she repositioned her coat over the personnel files. There was a reason she'd been assigned this case, and it had nothing to do with a missing woman. She had to be more careful around him. One mistake was all it would take to destroy her future with CBI. "Right."

The seconds ticked by in silence as one of the waitresses set a cup down in front of him and filled it before moving on to refill Campbell's. She didn't know what else to say, what to think. Her brain tried to convince her the man sitting across from her was nothing but a stranger, but her heart knew better. "It's nice to see the locals still come here after everything that happened."

"Is that why you showed up in the middle of my investigation? To talk about a diner that's seen better days?" Kendric took a slow pull of his coffee, the steam twisting and arching over scars that demanded attention.

"Would you rather talk about how I came off shift one night to find your side of the bed empty, your half of the closet cleaned out and a stack of cash on the kitchen table with a note that said 'I'm sorry'?" She hadn't meant to let the past infiltrate the present, but hiding the anger didn't mean it had gone away. It had just gotten more volatile.

"What do you want me to say, Campbell? We both know why I left like I did," he said.

The hell she did.

"You know, I'm a pretty good investigator, but even after all these years, I have no clue what I did to push you over the edge." Heat flared into her face. Her heart raced at the potential of confrontation, and there wasn't anything she could do to stop the escape of resentment she'd held on to all these years. "This is hard for me, too, you know. You think I wanted to be here? Do you think I wanted to step into your case or have to see you?"

"I saw what you thought of me after I came home from the hospital, Campbell. I saw the pity in your eyes." He pressed one finger into the table to enunciate the caged emotion he'd held back at the scene. "Every time you looked at me, your voice changed like I was some kind of wounded animal. You were there for me in the hospital and after I was discharged out of obligation, but you didn't want to be. You wanted out of our relationship just as much as I did. Only I was the one who had the courage to do something about it."

"I didn't…" Ice blistered through her veins and stole her intention to see this through. That… That wasn't what happened at all. "You wanted out?"

"You'd been pulling away before the bombing that turned me into…this, Campbell." The fight seemed to leave him just as it had left her. As quickly and as painfully as it had arrived.

"You were obviously miserable. What was I supposed to do?"

The urge to reach for him, to explain, outweighed her own self-control, and she set her free hand over his. Calloused tendons tightened beneath her touch. "The bombing had nothing to do with—"

"Dispatch to Hudson, the chief is in a mood." His radio staticked from its position over his left shoulder. The female voice—smooth as whiskey and full of personality—countered the battle-ready hardness in Kendric's neck and shoulders, and Campbell pulled back. She hadn't seen it before, but she couldn't unsee it now. Despite her claim to have moved on, he'd actually succeeded. Plain and simple. "Something about that CBI agent taking jurisdiction on our missing persons case like the cockroach she is."

A flash of that crooked smile threatened to melt any woman in the vicinity with a pulse. Kendric pinched the radio between his thumb and index finger, craning his head toward his shoulder. The effect intensified the strength running along his neck and arms and stopped her heart cold. "I'll give him a call, Mace. By the way, the cockroach says hi."

Mace. Short for Macie Barclay, Battle Mountain's one and only dispatcher. The nickname shouldn't have bothered her, but Campbell felt as though her emotions were on a roller coaster. Out of control and making her nauseous. So what if he had a nickname for someone he worked with closely these past couple of months? That was Kendric. Once upon a time, he'd had a nickname for everyone he knew, including her. Besides, it wasn't as though she had any say in his life now. He'd most likely dated since their breakup five years ago. It made sense, and she had no reason to be uncomfortable with that fact.

Still, it hurt to actually hear the change in his voice when he'd spoken to Macie. Softer around the edges, lighter. He used to talk to her like that. Not to mention Macie Barclay was so different from her. The bohemian redhead lived in a tree house, for crying out loud. If Kendric had set out to scrub Campbell from his life, he'd done a damn fine job.

Campbell collected her coat, hiding the files she'd been reviewing beneath it. Choosing the diner as home base hadn't been the best idea, but she couldn't pass up the enriched promise of coffee and chili cheese fries. "Seems you're a hot commodity."

Damn it. Why did her voice have to shake?

"Comes with the territory. The chief and Dr. Pascale just had a baby, his brother Easton is busy running the veteran rehab facility up the mountain, and Cree and Alma just ended a double shift." Kendric tugged his wallet from his back pocket, molding his uniform across his chest, and tossed a twenty on the table between them. "Someone's got to have a level head around here."

"You like it here." She didn't know where the thought had come from or why she'd felt the need to say the words out loud, but she couldn't deny them, either. So many things had changed since the last time they'd been face-to-face, to the point she wasn't sure she knew him at all. "I can tell."

"It's quieter out here." He scanned the diner and the faces he would've gotten to know since quitting his instructor position with the ATF. "Simpler. I feel like I can actually breathe for the first time since…"

Since the bombing.

She understood that. Because, in a weird turn of events, she felt the same way. Campbell slid from the booth and threaded both arms into her coat, careful not to drop the files. "Well, this cockroach needs to check in with her own CO. Thanks for the coffee."

"I'll walk you out." Kendric stepped into line behind her and followed her out into the wet, cold street. He tucked deeper into his own coat, nodding to her. "Full caseload?"

"Something like that." She gripped the files closer. "Let me know when Dr. Pascale gets back to you about Jane Doe's autopsy. I'd like to be there for the exam if possible." The devastating consequences of one bomber's choices sucker punched her in the gut as she took in the destruction along Main Street, but it was nothing compared to the pure heat of Kendric's attention. Right then, she couldn't help but liken the rebuilding of this small town to the reconstruction going on inside him, and it was then the theory of why he'd been drawn here in the first place surfaced. They were both broken. But not beyond repair. "I can drop you off at the station if you need."

"That would be hard considering it was blown up two months ago." He nodded toward the end of the street where backhoes and construction workers tried to sift through the blackened rubble. "Two devices. Gregson managed to decommission the first one. Missed the second. We're working out of the Whispering Pines Ranch outside of town for the time being."

"Sounds cozy." She turned to face the rental she'd picked up in Boulder.

And froze.

Confusion rippled through her as she studied the beautiful glass snow globe positioned on the hood of her SUV.

"I knew you had a thing for snow globes," he said. "Didn't think you'd have one mounted on the hood of your car."

"I didn't. It's a rental." Her throat dried. The gingerbread wonderland captured inside had come fully alive, as though someone had shaken the globe at the right moment, then simply walked away. Her gaze scanned the street, but she couldn't make sense of any distinct features. "I… I packed it in my luggage I left at the motel down the street."

She crammed her hand into her jacket, wedging her files into her rib cage. Faster than she meant to, she snapped a latex glove over her hand and reached for the globe.

A note fell at her feet, tucked underneath the ornament.

Kendric collected it and unfolded the creases. It was then she understood. He turned the note to face her, and the slanted handwriting came into focus. "Looks like Sabrina Bryon isn't the only one our kidnapper is interested in."

Chapter Three

Stop looking for her.

Those four words echoed on an endless loop in his head until he couldn't differentiate between his own thoughts and those of the bastard out to scare Campbell.

Kendric twisted the dead bolt of the front door and crossed the threshold. The alarm panel signaled warning, and he punched in the code to disarm it, all the while unable to shake the feeling of being watched. "Whoever took Sabrina Bryon knows you're investigating her disappearance. They've done their homework, they know your background and they're obviously not afraid to make a point. You'll be safe here."

Campbell hauled her overnight bag she'd collected from Cindy's Motel over one shoulder as she stepped inside. She stomped the snow from her heels and shook so much from her blazer it created a ring at her feet. The pink in her cheeks and at the end of her nose added a bite to flawless skin he'd barely held himself back from touching in the diner. The back of his hand still burned with the sensation of her skin pressed against his as though she'd branded him. In a way, she had, but allowing himself to give in would only put them right back where they'd ended. Closed off. Distant. Emotionally starved. "Be honest. Babysitting duty wasn't exactly your plan tonight."

No, it wasn't, but the last time he'd disobeyed a direct order from his commanding officer, he'd ended up flat on his back with a wall of fire breathing down on him.

"It's just temporary." Everything was. He'd learned that lesson the hard way. "Guest bedroom is down the hall to the left. The bathroom is across the hall from that. You're welcome to clean up and get settled before we figure out our next move."

She set her overnight bag at the door, that brilliant gaze taking everything in. Hands on narrow hips he could grip in both hands, Campbell studied every inch of the cabin as though strategizing a defense. His gut told him she wouldn't miss a single detail. It was what made her such a good detective, but having her in this place… He wanted to make a good first impression. He didn't know why. She hadn't been part of his life going on five years now, and he sure as hell didn't care what anyone thought of his lifestyle or choices. Decorative and otherwise. "Wow. This seems a little too nice for a safe house. You guys like to live large down here."

"It's mine." Kendric tossed his keys on the small table. The open two-story log living room demanded attention. He hadn't done much decorating in the short amount of time he'd relegated himself to staying in Battle Mountain, but the structure did what it was supposed to.

"This isn't a safe house?" Her gaze snapped to his, and a hint of the fire he'd once admired graveled her voice. "Kendric, what the hell are you thinking? Someone broke into my motel room and went through my personal effects to send a message, and your first thought was to bring me home?"

"Believe me, if I'd had any other choice, you wouldn't be here." At all. He left that last thought to settle between them, not in the mood to drive the invisible knife carving through him deeper. "You might be used to state and federal resources, but down here we're on our own. No safe houses. No forensic lab. No crime scene, homicide or missing persons units. It's me, a sleep-deprived chief of police, a part-time veteran rehab founder, a washed-out bomb squad tech and a rookie who barely survived her first case." He spread his arms wide to make a point. "Welcome to Battle Mountain, Detective. You're going to love it."

He headed for the kitchen and wrenched open the refrigerator. Every nerve in his body had been stripped raw from the moment he'd seen her in the middle of his crime scene. He needed a distraction. Prying the cap from a bottle of beer with his thumb, he swallowed a mouthful to take the edge off. Just for a little while.

Her knuckles threatened to break through the thin skin along the backs of her hands as she slid onto a barstool on the other side of the peninsula between them. "I can't imagine how difficult it must've been for your fellow officers to have to deal with those past cases on their own. Two spree killers, a serial killer. That ATF agent you knew. They're lucky to have you."

The sincerity in her expression stole the fight right out of him, and Kendric reached back into the fridge for an identical bottle. Her eyes widened at the offer, and he was rewarded with a thin smile and a nod of thanks. They weren't partners. Hell, they weren't even friends, but as long as they were assigned to work this case together, a small token of understanding was better than anything else he had to offer. The list of differences between them was just too damn long. Her ability to emotionally detach, fully commit and take a step back to get the larger picture had outgunned him from the beginning. It had just taken third-degree burns over ten percent of his body to show him the truth. Neither of them would change for the other.

He took another pull from his beer and settled back against the cold granite, watching her. "I'm just sorry I wasn't able to stop this place from going up in flames before it was too late."

"Does it get tiring?" she asked.

Confusion rippled through him. "What?"

"Taking on the weight of the world. Always assuming the responsibility of trying to fix everyone else's mistakes." She tipped the neck of her beer toward him and took a drink for herself. Sliding off her barstool, Campbell rounded the end of the counter, leaving her bottle behind. His pulse rocketed into his throat as she closed the distance between them. "You've been in law enforcement long enough to understand Agent Freehan's motive. She killed her sister out of jealousy. She set devices all over this town to hide the evidence and to make sure no one could identify her victim. She would've killed everyone if it had helped her get away with what she'd done. So why are you trying to convince yourself you're the one who triggered the explosives?"

Because in a way he had. Kendric finished the last of his beer, her intelligent, assessing gaze studying his every move. His heart slammed against his ribs as the truth clawed free from the box he'd tried to bury it in. "I taught her how to set those charges."

"You were an ATF instructor." Her shoulders hiked a bit higher as though that was enough to excuse what he'd done. "That was literally your job."

"No." He shook his head. "Christine—Agent Freehan—was with the agency for nearly fifteen years before I transferred from the sheriff's department. I taught her how to set the charges she used to kill her sister, to try to kill Officer Majors, the ones that nearly demolished this town."

"I don't... I don't understand." Campbell took a step back, and the part of him that had missed her, that wondered if he'd made the right choice, raged. "She'd spent years studying explosives. She would've known—"

"No. She came to me about a month before her sister was found in the bottom of a gulch not too far from here. Said she was working a case." His hands shook as a meaningless conversation between colleagues that had turned deadly played through his head. But it was more than that. He just hadn't wanted to admit his part. "A homicide victim who'd been killed with a small device but thoroughly enough that police hadn't been able to put the victim's body back together for an identification. She asked me what the device might look like, how much C-4 would be required to contain the blast, where the killer might've placed the explosive on the body. I hadn't heard of an open investigation with those specs, but it was my job to prepare the agents who came through my seminars for any possible scenario. I thought I was helping with an active case."

"Instead she was using you and your specs to design her own explosive." Not a question. Campbell folded her arms across her midsection. A habit she still hadn't broken after all these years, one she'd used a lot leading up to when he'd ended things. Like she was protecting herself against him, and he hated that. Hated that she couldn't be herself around him, that she had to lie to him, that she had to guard herself against him. But had he honestly given her any other choice? "I'm sorry. I didn't know.

None of that… None of that was in the official reports."

"I didn't know until it was too late." He wanted another beer, but drinking himself into false security wasn't going to do either of them any good. And it wouldn't bring Sabrina Bryon home or find Jane Doe's killer. Whether Kendric liked it or not, he and Campbell were the only ones equipped and trained to handle this caliber of a case.

"But because of you, Agent Freehan was apprehended." Campbell notched her chin a bit higher, countering her earlier escape. "You were the one Battle Mountain PD turned to when they got stuck in their investigation. You were the one they called in to handle transporting her into federal custody. You saved a lot of lives here. Shouldn't that count for something?"

"I'm not sure that's enough." He wasn't sure anything he did would be enough. Because it wasn't just about that conversation. It wasn't just about the havoc a colleague had caused here.

"Why wouldn't it be?" she asked. "Kendric, I understand why you might feel responsible, but Agent Freehan would've killed her sister one way or another. You cannot tell me you are responsible for what happened to this town.

Why are you doing this to yourself? What's keeping you here?"

"It doesn't matter." He couldn't get into this. Not with her. It wouldn't end the way she thought it would. Heading for the hallway leading to the bedroom wing of the cabin, he tried to shut down the shame, the guilt, the embarrassment from tearing through him all over again. It wasn't any use. Campbell had always known how to hit his buttons. Years of distance hadn't changed that.

"Yes, it does." She followed after him. "You came here for a reason, Kendric. You gave up an entire career with the sheriff's department in favor of your dream job with the ATF. I understand why what happened with Agent Freehan shook your confidence, but you left your family, your friends, everything you knew to play a small-town reserve officer with no experience with serial killers or homicide investigations. For what? Because of some distorted responsibility to a town you've never seen?"

"To protect them from me!" Kendric turned on her. She flinched under the severity of his tone, and he instantly regretted losing his temper. The outburst echoed off the two-story opening of the living room and shook him straight to his core. Then again, hostility was always what he'd done best. It was the only way to make sure no other emotions could escape, but the truth wouldn't die. No matter how many times he'd tried to suffocate it.

The bitterness, the anger that came with having his entire world ripped out from beneath him in an instant simmered just below the surface, but he was better than this. He was better trained than this. Repression had become an old friend these past few years, and he called on it now. Only it wasn't enough. The wound had been opened, and there was no turning back. Not from Campbell. The last of his air reserves escaped his lungs. "Because they deserved to be free of the obligation to help a defective has-been who couldn't even see a threat when it was right in front of him. And so do you."

EVERY MINUTE SABRINA BRYON was missing increased the search area, but none of that mattered as she considered Kendric's words.

He'd left to free her from caring about him. To free everyone who'd loved him.

The narrow hallway closed in around her. It had been different before, listening to him talk to the Battle Mountain PD dispatcher. Her own insecurities had taken a public conversation and inflamed the hurt she'd carried all these years. Because it hadn't been tangible.

This… This was different. This was real. She could see his pain. Feel it. Hear the strain in his voice, and she hated every second it squeezed her lungs until there was nothing left.

The explosion that had ripped apart his life and his body hadn't been a one-time event.

He was still living those horrifying seconds. Every single day while the rest of the world moved on. Campbell took a step toward him. "Listen to me, because I'm only going to say this once, Kendric Hudson. You're not defective. You're not a has-been. The voices in your head telling you otherwise have been lying to you, isolating you from the people who can help. They've been forcing you to relive the same nightmare all these years, and they're very good at it, but you're stronger than them. You just can't see it yet."

He didn't answer, didn't even seem to breathe. The small muscles along his jaw flexed under pressure. He'd heard her loud and clear, but in the end, he'd have to be the one to do something about it. Because she wasn't part of his life anymore.

They had a case, a missing young mother, and a Jane Doe taking up space in a funeral home. Compartmentalize. Detach. She'd gotten so good at it over the years. What was one more time? Campbell cleared her throat.

"You know, I think I'm going to take you up on freshening up before we come up with an investigative plan. There's still mud in my heels, and I don't want to risk spreading it through your house. Excuse me."

She maneuvered past him—to escape, to hide. Because there was no way in hell she'd let him see what came next. He'd been the love of her life. He'd been her greatest supporter for a time, but she couldn't force him to see the truth. No matter how much she wanted to fight this battle for him, she had two investigations to unravel.

"I never stopped thinking about you," he said.

She swiped at her face before turning to face him, mere feet from the guest bedroom that promised a space to get herself under control. She couldn't work like this. She couldn't investigate a homicide and a kidnapping and carry out CBI's orders while the past kept puncturing through the present. She couldn't go back to Denver empty-handed, and staying here, working with Kendric—losing herself in him all over again—wasn't a risk she was willing to take. Not anymore. "We all have choices we regret."

"I don't regret a single minute of you." The use of his nickname for her triggered a chain reaction of familiarity and comfort she hadn't felt in years. One word. That was all it had taken to stop her in her tracks. Kendric slid his hands into his uniform slacks. "When I left, I tried to forget you. I did everything I could to get you out from beneath my skin. I transferred to the ATF. I found a new apartment you hadn't stepped foot inside. I dated anyone who didn't look like you, but none of it worked."

Campbell reached for the practiced distance she'd coached herself through before getting into her rental and putting herself back in this position. "I'm not sure what you expect me to say to that."

"I couldn't scrub you from my life. No matter how many times I tried. You were always there." His throat convulsed with an exaggerated swallow. "With them…it wasn't like it was with you. I couldn't be myself with anyone. I thought I knew what was best, but I wasn't happy. Not like I was with you, and I have been kicking myself every minute of every day since I walked out that door."

Her heart jerked in her chest. The urge to reach out again—to test the limits of their partnership, to test herself—exploded through her. But what scared her the most was how much she wanted to touch him. She'd spent the past few years numbing herself to rejection and pain and loss, but for the first time since he'd left, she actually felt that physical weight he'd put on his shoulders. Heavy, suffocating, crushing. It was an impossible expectation for one person to suffer on their own. How had he done it all these months?

Kendric took a step forward, then another. For every foot of distance closed between them, her chest tightened, and before she understood his intentions, he'd wrapped his arms around her waist.

The combination of woodsmoke and dirt dived into her lungs and filled the farthest recesses of her senses. The muscles down her spine only hardened in defense while the hollowness she'd tried to ignore waned. She closed her eyes despite the storm of anger at herself for letting him get close, and her hands splayed across his back. Peaks and valleys of muscle and scar tissue rippled under her palms, and her guard slipped a little more.

"I'm glad you're here." His rushed exhalation tickled the underside of her chin a split second before she surrendered. Securing his hands at her back, he held on to her as though she were the only thing anchoring him to the earth. In that instant, he wasn't the annoyed reserve officer she'd met in the middle of a crime scene this morning. He was Kendric, the one who'd committed to making her smile every day, who'd laughed along with her at life's absurdities and pushed her to climb the investigative ladder outside of the sheriff's department. His inhalations matched her own as the minutes ticked by, and after so many years of wondering what she'd done wrong or if she'd been able to help him get through the aftermath of the bombing, she found herself not wanting this to end.

"Do you know what I was thinking about the other day? That house in Loveland." She could picture it now, so clearly. The dirt front yard, the broken chain-link fence. The hole in the roof after a bomber had made a mistake building his device and killed himself in the process. It was their first case together. "The lime-green one with red brick."

Kendric pried himself from her but kept his hands secured on her waist. One corner of his mouth hiked higher, giving the impression of a smile, but he'd obviously been out of practice for too long. "You mean the crime scene where you asked me out."

"Took some convincing. Especially since you were trying to clear everyone out of the house before it collapsed in on itself." Her laugh escaped easier than it had in years.

Lighter, freeing. "But I didn't give up. Because I knew we were going to make a good team."

"We did." The familiarity between them drained from his expression, and sooner than she wanted, he stepped free from her personal space. "For a while, at least."

Her gut twisted at the physical and emotional distance he'd weaponized so quickly. The uncertainty she'd become all too comfortable with returned, and Campbell scrambled to pull herself back together. They'd gotten through the first hurdle, but the hurt wouldn't be placated so easily. "Yeah. For a while."

"I'm going to find us something to eat while you clean up." He turned as he backed away. "Should only be a few minutes."

Was this how it would always be between them? One of them trying to leave while the other tried to get them to stay? Were things so bad between them it had really come to this eternal tug-of-war they couldn't escape? "Back in the diner, you said I was pulling away before the bombing, that I was miserable."

"We've got a case, Campbell." Kendric pulled a box of pasta from the pantry, followed up by an array of mushrooms, tomatoes and spinach from the fridge. "We're not going to solve everything between us tonight."

"You were right. I was miserable, but not because it had anything to do with you. I wanted to be there for you. I did, especially after the bombing. You needed me, but I didn't know how to… I didn't want to add to your stress while you were recovering," she said. "I didn't think you could handle it, and by the time I was ready to tell you the truth, you were gone. You wouldn't answer any of my calls, you'd blocked my emails and messages. I even tried to reach you through your parents, but you never answered back."

"What are you talking about?" Dark eyebrows drew together as he turned to face her.

"I was pregnant." The truth ground the last bit of fight from her bones, leaving nothing but emptiness and exhaustion. "Around eight weeks. I'd found out a week before the bombing. I had this whole surprise party planned for you for when you got home, but then your CO called to tell me what had happened."

"You were pregnant." The words barely registered between them in that too-narrow kitchen. Kendric scrubbed a hand through his hair as shock slapped the color from his face. "So when you recognized that pillow found by Jane Doe's body, it's because you…you have personal experience." Green eyes snapped to hers as his voice hardened. "We've been together all day, and you're just telling me this now?"

"I wanted to wait until the right moment." She shook her head as though the action could rewind the past few minutes, but there was no running from it this time. She'd started this. She had to see it through. "You revealed a personal secret. I figured it was my turn."

Kendric stumbled back as if she'd physically struck him. His Adam's apple dipped and rose on a strong swallow as the silence closed in. "We have a baby?"

"She's not a baby anymore. She just turned four. Her name is Penny. She stays with my parents when I'm on assignment. I can show you a picture." Campbell unpocketed her badge, careful to bend her credentials beneath the leather, and exposed the smiling blonde beauty behind the clear plastic window on the other side. The one who looked just like her dad but had been blessed with her mom's blond hair and blue eyes. "The pregnancy was hard. Especially at the beginning."

His hand shook as he took the picture from her. "She's beautiful."

"She's also very intense." Campbell took a step forward. "Do you understand now? I tried to hold it together for you, Kendric. I tried to be what you needed me to be. I really did, but learning about the bombing and the baby and dealing with the physical problems that came with her… I couldn't. I understand why you felt I wasn't there for you when you needed me the most. Because I wasn't. You leaving… it nearly broke me, but I was willing to hold on to us." Her heart threatened to beat straight out of her chest. "Why weren't you?"

"Dispatch to Hudson." Macie Barclay's incoming interruption from the radio at his shoulder destroyed his chance to answer. "Please respond."

Kendric locked that unreadable gaze on the photo as reality broke through the walls they'd built around them. He handed back her badge and answered. "This is Hudson. Go ahead."

"The chief found Sabrina Bryon's vehicle out on the Alpine Loop. You're going to want to get there as soon as you can." The channel fractured over broken radio waves. "Oh, and please be advised it's on fire."

Chapter Four

Flames had blackened the cliff face containing the fire to the road.

The Alpine Loop's circular route navigated through the high elevation of Cinnamon Pass and Engineer Pass in the San Juan Mountains, connecting Silverton, Ouray and Battle Mountain. Sharp peaks, withered tree growth and deep valleys demanded attention from every angle. Kendric hadn't ever seen anything like it. With snow already working its way down the surrounding mountains, the isolated one-lane dirt road had been the perfect location to destroy evidence. No tourists taking advantage of the views this time of year. Slowed cargo shipping. No witnesses.

Campbell rounded the hood of the SUV and approached ahead of him.

Mud squished under his boots as Kendric caught sight of Battle Mountain's chief of police, Weston Ford.

The sleepy town of less than a thousand residents hadn't had much in the way of a police department. At least, not until Chief Ford had scrounged together a solid team over the past year. He and his brother Easton, the town's second reserve officer, had brought down not one but two serial killers in a span of months in addition to taking on Kendric's former colleague from the ATF. Together, they'd protected Battle Mountain with a fraction of the resources he'd relied on during his career and given this town a reason to believe in heroes. The chief craned his head over his shoulder, backlit by the smoldering remains of what was left of Sabrina Bryon's sedan.

A few days' worth of beard growth intensified the sharp angles of the man's oval face, accentuated by the shade thrown by his ten-gallon hat. Dirt and ash clung to the new father's dark T-shirt hugging an athletic frame and washed the color from the chief's jeans. Despite the lower temperatures at this elevation, sweat trickled from Weston's short dark hair as he sidestepped to give Kendric and Campbell a view of the vehicle. "Just in time. Fire and rescue just gave us the all clear to take a look."

"Did you find any remains?" Campbell snapped a pair of gloves over her hands and approached the steaming blackened frame of the vehicle. Instantly focused on the task at hand.

Kendric circled around the front of the car toward the driver's side.

"No, but considering how long the wreckage was burning before it was spotted and the amount of accelerant we can smell from here, my guess is if there was, there won't be any evidence of them now." Chief Ford extended a work-gloved hand. "You must be the investigator from the CBI. Weston Ford."

"Campbell Dwyer. Who spotted the fire?" Campbell didn't even seem to acknowledge the chief as anything more than a potential resource, her entire being consumed with finding answers.

"A private passenger plane flying over radioed in." The chief lowered his hand, settling a suspicious gaze on Kendric as Campbell got closer to the vehicle's remains. "They ended up circling until fire and rescue arrived on scene to keep an eye on it and make sure the blaze didn't spread. The last thing this town needs is another round of evacuations. Lucky for us, most of the trees up here have given up the ghost for winter."

"I don't see any other vehicle tracks leading away from the scene. No gas cans, either." Campbell straightened, moving slowly along the length of the cremated car. "Whoever set the fire most likely used the gasoline from the vehicle itself to start it. This doesn't look premeditated. The kidnapper improvised to make a clean getaway." She pointed to the ground, trailing her finger along the flattened grass lining the edge of an open cliff on the other side of the road. "Whoever it was used the grass to hide their shoe impressions."

Hell, she'd read all that in under a minute. Admiration simmered under his skin as Kendric caught the slight narrowing of her gaze. A bomb could've gone off right then, and Campbell still wouldn't have shifted her focus. Even on his best days, Kendric and his team would've taken hours of surveying a scene before coming up with any kind of conclusions. She was good at this, and Sabrina Bryon was lucky as hell to have Campbell on her trail.

"Fire and rescue said the same thing, but that's not all. Your perp has definitely done their homework, maybe even trained in forensics. I found pieces of a duffel bag in the back seat. Torched but intact enough for us to prove there were two sets of clothes as well as some toiletries and a pair of boots inside." The chief headed for a blue tarp spread out along the ground highlighting different scraps of evidence. "Looks like the kidnapper had

Sabrina Bryon change into clean clothes before destroying the rest." Weston unpocketed a
pen and gathered up a stained scrap of fabric.

This was all starting to feel too familiar.

"You're thinking this might be another law
enforcement officer." Kendric's gut clenched.
He hadn't wanted to voice the theory, but after
what these townspeople and this department
had already been through, they couldn't discount the possibility. Agent Freehan had swept
into this town on the back of surviving two
serial killers, and taken every last ounce of
safety from Battle Mountain. He couldn't let
it happen again. "Knowledge of forensics and
protocols?"

"I'm not sure yet." The chief nodded, his
expression more grave than a moment before. "Chloe's going to try to run DNA from
what's left of these clothes. See if we can get
a match. But as of right now we've got a missing woman, a gunshot victim who looks a hell
of a lot like her pretending to be pregnant and
a frantic husband who might not make it out
of surgery. What the hell is going on here?"

Pops and hisses of dying embers broke
through the low whistle of wind whipping
through the valley. Heat flared along Kendric's neck as he took in the damage. "An affair gone wrong?"

"Elliot Bryon sought a lover who looked identical to his wife and asked her to role-play a pregnancy?" Campbell asked. "In my experience, when a man is stepping out on his pregnant wife, finding someone who looks like her isn't his highest priority."

"Or our Jane Doe's significant other discovered her secret. Figured he could get back at the man sleeping with his wife by taking Sabrina." Kendric reviewed the list of friends and family associated with the Bryon family. It would take days to interview them all with his limited amount of manpower on this case. Hell. Twelve hours into this investigation, there were still too many unanswered questions, and without Jane Doe's identity, he didn't know if they'd make any headway in finding answers. "Either way, we won't get anywhere until we can talk to the husband."

"I'll check in with the hospital." The chief pulled his cell from his back pocket. "You two stay on this. The kidnapper destroyed this car because they knew it could lead us back to them. I want it all pulled apart and searched." Weston headed back toward his vehicle down the road, leaving Campbell and Kendric alone.

"Gasoline burns at fifteen hundred degrees. Any DNA the kidnapper or Sabrina left behind wouldn't have survived." Kendric rounded to the back of the vehicle. Twisted metal steamed as the sun dipped behind the cliff face. They didn't have but a couple more hours before evening hit. Whatever they needed to do, they needed to do it now.

Campbell didn't answer, didn't even seem to breathe, as she stared at the charcoaled remains. "This is the victim's car."

"According to Macie, the VIN number matches to the registration from the DMV. Same make and model, too," he said. "Why does that matter?"

"We never found another set of vehicle tracks leading to the Bryon home apart from the victims' vehicles. This one and Elliot Bryon's pickup, which you'd already searched. At first, I thought the kidnapper and Jane Doe had come from the tree line. Maybe with an ATV or a dirt bike, but Gregson and Majors haven't found anything that supports that theory."

Hell, she was right. And he hadn't seen it before now. The smoke from burned leather and metal drove into his lungs, singeing the back of his throat. "All right. So how did the abductor get to the Bryon home?"

"Let's assume you were right before. Jane Doe and Elliot Bryon are having an affair. He brings her to the cabin for a rendezvous while his wife is out of the house, but surprise, Sabrina Bryon comes home early and catches him in the act." A humorless laugh escaped full pink lips and broke the connection between the hardened investigator and the woman he hadn't been able to sanitize from his life.

"Okay. She's upset. They're expecting a baby, so emotions are already running high, and she's just learned her husband is having another woman role-play a pregnancy. A woman who looks frighteningly just like her." He followed the curve of the burned-out vehicle until he and Campbell stood on the same side, and something deep inside aligned with her. "Something goes wrong. They argue. Sabrina's either brought a gun with her or she knows where Elliot stores his. Jane Doe is shot in the process."

"Jane Doe escapes. Sabrina can't keep up with her because of the pregnancy, so she shoots her husband's mistress from a distance, hitting Jane Doe in the back. Then focuses on her husband. She shoots him, and Sabrina flees with the murder weapon, a change of clothes and toiletries and her vehicle." Campbell had somehow masterfully fit the pieces together, but it was only the beginning. Raising her gaze to his, she seemed to snap out of her own internal study. "What background information have we pulled on Sabrina Bryon?"

"The basics. Financials, employment history, driving records, cell phone data." Anything included in the standard protocol when someone went missing. "From what we can tell, she doesn't have any living relatives. No debt. She moved here a few years ago, married Elliot Bryon within a year. Macie said it was in all the papers. Kind of like a Cinderella story. Elliot Bryon comes from money. Something to do with a family-owned business. Sabrina had been struggling finding work. They met, and it was happily-ever-after since. All that was about two years ago."

"Where did she move from?" The slight octave change in Campbell's voice said the story didn't line up for her. "Did she go to school? Was she married previously?"

"I'll have to dig deeper when I get back to the temporary headquarters at the ranch." Kendric caught himself comparing the photo she'd showed him of their daughter to the missing persons agent in front of him. Same shade of blue in their eyes, same texture of hair. Beautiful. She met his gaze head-on, and a different kind of heat altogether burned through him. He did know one thing for certain. Campbell wasn't going anywhere. Whether he liked it or not, they were in this together. "Why? What are you thinking?"

"Whoever shot Elliot Bryon put two in his chest center mass. That's nearly impossible if you've never handled a weapon before. And whoever burned this vehicle did so to destroy DNA and any chance of forensics recovery. Civilians, especially those who are scared and on the run, don't stop to think about things like that." She pointed to the car. "I'm thinking Sabrina Bryon isn't who she convinced everyone she is."

Shock nearly knocked Kendric back a step. "Then who the hell is she?"

THE SCENT OF fire and gasoline clung to her coat as she stripped it from her shoulders. Night had fallen, shutting down any chance of searching Sabrina Bryon's vehicle further without the support of floodlights. There hadn't been much left, as Kendric had theorized. The gasoline had all but eviscerated any evidence that would've helped their case. With Easton Ford securing the scene overnight, they'd have to wait until morning to pick up where they'd left off.

How did a town like Battle Mountain manage to solve any kind of investigation with the limited manpower and resources they had?

Well, that was why she was really here, wasn't it? To unearth the source of the evil closing in around this town over the past year.

Campbell peeled mud-crusted heels from her aching feet and tossed them onto the floor. The room Kendric had lent her since her motel room had been raided was simple. Just like him. Little decor, neutral colors, clean aesthetic. No personal photos or signs he'd made this a home, but the way he talked about this town said he never intended to go back to Denver. Maybe not even for his daughter. She wasn't sure how she felt about that. She and Penny had been fine on their own all these years, but now that Kendric knew of their child's existence, she'd expected…more. Curiosity. Maybe even desire to meet Penny.

The queen-size bed called her on a deep, exhaustion-heavy level, and Campbell stripped free from the rest of her clothing to keep odor transfer to a minimum. She needed a shower. A hot meal. Twenty hours of sleep. To hear Penny's voice.

She tugged her credentials from her blazer pocket and pulled the photo of her daughter free. After setting it upright against the nightstand lamp, she donned her sleepwear—an oversize shirt and a pair of sweats—and headed for the kitchen. Her stomach growled as though sensing sustenance nearby.

"I can hear your stomach coming from a mile away." A low laugh permeated through the dim lighting above the kitchen table. Kendric raised his gaze from the shuffled paperwork in front of him. "I take it you're hungry."

"Sorry for interrupting. Apparently cheese fries aren't very filling." She pointed to the refrigerator. "You mind?"

He nodded permission. "No apology needed. I stopped being able to see the reports an hour ago." Scrubbing his face, he looked as tired as she felt in that moment, but it was nothing compared to the last look she'd had of him in Denver. "At this point, I couldn't even tell you what time that clock over the stove says."

"Thanks." A cool burst of air slammed against her overheated face and neck as she searched the fridge. Bare. Just like the rest of the house, but a block of cheddar cheese in one of the drawers promised to ease her craving for comfort food. "Sounds like you could use one of my famous grilled cheese sandwiches."

Kendric sat back in his chair at the kitchen table. "I'd give up my right arm for one of them right about now."

"You got it." It was hard to fight the smile hooking her mouth at both corners. She'd almost forgotten how charming he could be at times. She set to work and moved through the kitchen as though she owned the place, the pressure of his gaze sliding between her shoulder blades. If she was being honest with herself, she'd missed the easiness they could fall into. She'd missed him.

"Whose name is on Penny's birth certificate?" he asked.

Tension replaced the smile lingering on her mouth. She forced the butcher knife down through the block of cheese, trying not to slice her fingers off. They hadn't been given the time to slow down since discovering Sabrina Bryon had gone missing, but she owed him answers. "Yours."

"Gotta say, that's not the answer I was expecting." His voice dipped, barely rising above a whisper.

Campbell set down the knife and turned to face him. "I was never trying to keep her from you, Kendric. I wanted to make it as easy as possible for you if you decided you wanted to be part of our lives. You're the one who refused to have any kind of contact with me."

"I know." He swiped his empty mug off the table and shoved back in his chair. Pulling open one of the overhead cabinets in the small U-shaped layout, he brushed against her hip as he pulled a loaf of bread free. Electricity shot through her side, fighting the tightness in her muscles as he set the bag on the counter and filled his coffee cup. "I just meant... I figured you would've wanted someone else. Gotten married, had him adopt her and take his last name. Made yourself a family."

Her mouth dried as the waves of warmth spread through her. One touch. That was all it had taken to ratchet her nerves into overdrive, and Campbell squeezed her hand firmly around the knife to finish what she'd started. She sliced through a few more pieces of cheese and unpacked four pieces of bread, arranging it all. "Families come in all shapes and sizes. What Penny and I have is all I need."

"Yeah." Kendric shifted his weight between both feet, taking a sip of dark roast with just a hint of cinnamon in the air. "Tell me about her. Our...daughter."

"That word isn't typically used as a swear word, but sure. Um, well her pediatrician is worried about my mental health." A lightness penetrated through the violence and uncertainty that had fisted in her gut throughout the day. "She refuses to eat meat and loves broccoli. Anything green, actually."

"Broccoli?" His face twisted into hard lines just as Penny's did when she wouldn't accept no for an answer, and Campbell couldn't help but laugh. "Are you sure she's mine? What kid actually likes broccoli?"

"This one." She assembled the sandwiches, smearing butter with a good helping of garlic powder from one of the drawers on the outsides. "She loves imaginary play. She can make any two items talk to each other. The other day she'd found two straws in the car. Before I knew it, one was accusing the other of sneaking a cookie from the pantry and had gotten sent to time-out."

His deep laugh resonated through her, creeping under the wall she'd built over the past few years to protect herself from him. "She sounds amazing."

"She is." Campbell set the sandwiches in the pan, and the scent of cheese filled the small space between them. "Her confidence is off the charts. I keep telling my mom she's either going to be a CEO or a serial killer."

"Why not both?" he asked.

"You have a point." She turned to grab for a spatula across the counter, stopping short.

Kendric held one out, and in that moment, he seemed so much…bigger. More real. More… attainable. The bitterness he'd become all too comfortable with had melted from his voice and released the anger from his expression.

Right then, he resembled the man she'd fallen in love with all those years ago. Her partner.

His gaze dipped to her lips a split second before he closed the distance between them.

His mouth crushed to hers.

He speared one hand into her hairline. Desperate to keep her from backing away? Her breath mixed with his as she savored the bite of black coffee and man. Lean muscle backed her against the refrigerator and held her upright. Instinctively, she opened her mouth to give him better access, and he deepened the kiss as though trying to prove something to both of them. His heart pounded against her chest, unsteady but strong. Every sweep of his tongue worked to undo the guard she'd built between them until Campbell wasn't sure where he started and she ended.

Then pain seared down her front.

"Oh my gosh! Hot, hot, hot!" Stepping back, she fanned her shirt with both hands. The thin, vintage-feel fabric burned her midsection and thighs as coffee slid down her body.

"Oh, crap. Here. Let me." He set the mug on the counter and reached for a dish towel in the same move. Crouching, Kendric moved to get as much of the coffee from her legs and feet before the burns set in.

"That's… That's okay. I can do it." Campbell

ducked to take the towel from him but failed to dodge his skull as he straightened. Pain exploded across her face, and she fell back against the refrigerator. Lightning flashed across her vision, her eyes watering from impact.

Kendric gripped the back of his head. "Hell, woman. You could've just said no. You didn't have to beat me to make a point."

"At least you're not the one bleeding." She tipped her head back to contain the blood flow from her nose. "Could you get me a paper towel?"

"Damn it." Kendric ripped a clean towel from the stand, soaked one corner in cold water and faced her. "Let me see."

"I think you've done enough damage for one night." Mentally and physically. Campbell shook her head, unable to hold back the absurdity of the past couple of minutes. It was just like them to turn a heated, passionate moment into chaos. "It'll stop in a minute."

"And until then, I can make sure nothing is broken." He set his free hand along the side of her neck, tipping her head back gently with his thumb.

Her pulse thudded hard as she followed directions, and the gravity of this moment—of them being in the same room after all these years—set in. She wasn't sure if she'd ever see him again, and now they'd been assigned to work a missing persons case with more questions than answers.

"I'm sorry," he said.

She stared up into the canned lights as he pressed the wet towel beneath her nose. "It was an accident, Officer Hudson. I won't be pressing charges."

"Not about the bloody nose." He dabbed at her nose and mouth. "Well, yes, about the bloody nose, but also about before. That you felt you couldn't tell me you were pregnant because you didn't think I could handle it on top of everything else. Funny thing is, you were probably right."

An apology. Her heart squeezed harder than it should have. "To be fair, you had a lot on your mind at the time."

"More than what was left on my face." His attempt at sarcasm fell flat, and the reality of their situation solidified. He'd walked out on her without warning. There was no argument or excuse. He'd hurt her and deprived Penny of a father's influence. "I wish I could go back. Change things. If I'd just done the job I was hired to do—"

"Stop." Campbell set her hand over his, taking the paper towel. She tipped her head forward and swiped the last of the blood from her face. "You almost died, Kendric. If Cree Gregson hadn't tackled you to the floor when that second bomb had gone off, you wouldn't even be here. I know it doesn't feel like it, but I'm grateful. You're alive. That's more than what a lot of ordinance techs can say. You still have a choice about how you want to live your life. Is it going to be here, where you're haunted by the devastation wreaked by your colleague, or in Denver, where your friends and family are waiting for you to come home? Where your daughter is waiting to meet her dad?"

He didn't answer, didn't even seem to breathe, and it was then she knew. For him, there was no choice. The man he'd been didn't exist anymore. The life he'd had didn't exist anymore. He'd cut himself off from anything and everyone that connected him to that time. Including her. Only in the end, he'd be the one to suffer, and her heart broke a little more.

"You were so angry about the bombing that you wouldn't talk to anyone. Not even the people in your unit. Not to me." She raised her hand to frame the side of his face, and he flinched. From her. Her gut clenched at the loss of the passionate, uncontained man he'd been a moment ago. The one who'd helped her forget the world with a single kiss. "You're still angry about it. I can hear it in your voice."

Kendric backed into the opposite counter, trapped in his own kitchen. Nowhere to run. Nowhere to hide. It was just the two of them and a long list of mistakes they'd made together over the years.

Cold worked through her as the coffee cooled. There wasn't a single brain cell in her head capable of processing what had happened between them the past few minutes. Sensory overload and exhaustion had already started forcing her body to shut down. "We were always better at managing our careers than our personal lives, weren't we?" She pointed to the smoking pan a few feet away. "You're going to want to flip the sandwiches before they burn."

She didn't wait for an answer this time as she headed back toward her room, losing her appetite. In truth, considering why she'd really come to Battle Mountain, she couldn't afford to hear one.

Chapter Five

He'd made a mistake.

Kissing Campbell. Wishing things had
turned out differently for both of them. Eating both of their grilled cheese sandwiches.
Obsessing about his and Campbell's conversation last night hadn't helped one bit. Kendric
tried to hold in a yawn, failing miserably, as he
shuffled into the kitchen. She'd wanted an answer. She'd wanted him to tell her he planned
to head back to Denver, to pick up where they
left off and be part of his daughter's life.

But he couldn't.

That little girl—vegetarian or not—deserved
better than him for a father. Campbell deserved
better than a broken ghost of himself. What
she wanted, what their daughter needed…he
couldn't give. Maybe not ever.

Movement registered from the living room.

"Didn't realize you were already up." He

scrounged for a clean mug and poured himself a fresh cup of coffee.

"I'm on the there's-a-child-in-my-bed-at-five-a.m.-watching-cartoons schedule. Hard to kick." She swiped her fingers expertly over the laptop trackpad balanced in the middle of her crossed legs. She'd changed since he'd dumped nearly an entire cup of hot coffee on her chest, but the outfit was made up of the same pieces. T-shirt and sweatpants. And damn if having her so relaxed in the middle of his living room wasn't the sexiest thing he'd ever seen.

Kendric cleared the morning dryness from his throat. "Campbell, about last night—"

"I've composed a list of Sabrina Bryon's closest friends in town based off her phone records. There hasn't been any activity since she disappeared and the phone is turned off to keep us from triangulating a signal, but if she's on the run, she'll go somewhere familiar for help. I think I've narrowed it down to the most likely person based off her call history. The number is registered to a Chelsea Ingar." She set the laptop on an old wood end table he'd taken off Gregson's hands when the reserve officer had moved in with his partner, Alma. "Give me about thirty minutes to shower and dress, and I'll be ready to go."

The detachment was back in her voice, and

Kendric mentally kicked himself for screwing this up. "Wait. Please."

"It's fine, Kendric. I didn't come here to try to bring you back to Denver, and to be honest, I shouldn't have said anything in the first place." She moved to push past him, but he held his ground. Swiping her hand under her slightly bruised nose, she pulled up short. She stretched a hand toward him, enunciating her next words. "You don't owe me answers. Really, you don't owe me anything, and it was out of line for me to expect you to explain yourself. Besides, we have a case. We're good. I promise."

"No, we're not. We're not even close to being good." He fisted one hand as the past threatened to consume the present. Images of fire and pain and death wouldn't recede, but keeping them bottled up all these years hadn't helped, either. "You don't know what it was like. Lying in that hospital bed, being able to see, hear and feel everything but not having the ability to do anything about it. My throat was so burned from the explosion, I couldn't even scream when the nurses changed my bandages. I couldn't move. I couldn't be touched."

Campbell dropped her gaze to the floor, crossing her arms over her lean frame. "I'm sorry. That sounds…miserable and terrifying."

"Gregson got it worse, but he can hide the scars. I can't." The dead nerves along the right side of his face tingled with phantom sensation. "I can still feel my skin slipping when I let myself stop long enough to think about what happened. I can still hear Gregson's screams in my nightmares, knowing there was nothing I could do to help either of us. I was the team leader on that assignment, Campbell. I disobeyed an order to evacuate because I thought I could get to the device before it went off. I was supposed to protect my team, and I failed. And you…you're telling me I have the choice about how I live the rest of my life, that I can just go back to Denver to be with my friends and family. To be with my daughter. But the truth is, I don't. Because any life they would have with me isn't a life worth living."

Shock snapped her gaze to his, and Campbell stepped forward. "That's not true. You—"

"I can't give you what you want, Campbell. What's more is I can't be the father that little girl deserves. Not with this face and with all the stuff that comes with it. So I'm not coming back." He motioned to the waves of scar tissue contorting his face. Kendric countered her approach, but voicing the deepest fears he'd kept to himself all this time was freeing in a way.

Acceptance was the first step. Wasn't that what they said? He retreated for the hallway. "Ever."

"You're wrong, you know. You're not broken, Kendric. You're not defective or any less lovable because of what you've been through, and I feel sorry that you've accepted that's the only path for you. Because you have so much to offer. More than you can possibly understand." Her voice softened. "I only hope you realize it before it's too late."

His grip tightened around his mug. "I don't need your pity, Campbell. Just your experience with missing victims to solve this case."

"Then I guess we better get moving. According to GPS, Chelsea Ingar is home right now. The victim's phone records put them in contact several times a day over the past few years. She might be able to give us more insight into Sabrina's life while we wait to hear from the ob-gyn." The floorboards creaked in protest as she made her way down the hall in front of him before she disappeared behind the solid wood door of the guest bedroom.

Kendric retreated to his own room and went about his normal routine. The hot water ran out halfway through scrubbing the scent of burnt rubber and dirt from his skin and beard. Just as well. Every second he and Campbell wasted on trying to hash out the differences between them was another second Sabrina Bryon wasn't on her way home, and he couldn't allow his personal life to obstruct this investigation. Neither of them could. He dressed in full uniform, securing his weapon in the holster on his hip, and stepped out into the hallway.

The sound of water hitting tile reached his ears. Campbell hadn't finished in the guest bathroom, but he couldn't imagine her shower was any warmer than his. He had every intention of stalking past her bedroom without so much as a glance inside to honor her privacy, but a small rectangle set upright on the nightstand caught his attention.

The photo Campbell had showed him last night. Penny.

His shoes scuffed against the hardwood as though the smiling four-year-old had some invisible rope tied around his waist to pull him closer. Before he realized what he was doing, Kendric picked up the photo for a closer look. A waterfall of blond hair cascaded around a heart-shaped face, soft and shiny and a little bit frizzed. Big blue eyes stared straight ahead as Penny charged toward the camera with two giant fistfuls of multicolored leaves. She was poised to attack, ready to take on everyone and anything that got in her way. The photo had probably been taken a couple months ago—a mere glimpse into a life he'd never have—but Kendric felt as though she were right there. With him.

"She has your smile," she said.

His nerves flinched at the sound of Campbell's voice behind him. He hadn't heard her leave the bathroom, and he quickly replaced the photo where she'd positioned it on the nightstand. "I didn't mean to invade your privacy. I just…" He didn't know the end to that sentence. "Hell, I don't know what I was doing. Sorry."

"Once I had four nurses, an ob-gyn and a medical student witness a baby come out of my vagina, I lost any need for privacy." Campbell dumped her pajamas and toiletries onto the bed beside her unzipped duffel bag, whose bottom was lined by a stack of manila folders. The same files she'd tried to hide from him at the diner. She quickly repacked her bag. "On top of that, Penny thinks breasts are the greatest thing on the planet, and she tries to get to mine every chance she can. Even in public."

"To be fair, she's not wrong." He caught himself envisioning the exact image she'd described and wanted to kick his own ass for his hypocrisy. He'd made it clear he couldn't be part of her and Penny's lives, but his imagination had yet to get the message. "I'll, uh, let you finish getting ready and meet you at the car."

"No need." Securing her sidearm at her hip, Campbell flared her blazer—this one a deep gray—and buttoned up. Tendrils of wet blond hair slipped free from her shoulders, and he wanted nothing more than to thread his hand into the strands all over again. "We can go."

"Lead the way." Within minutes, he was behind the wheel with Campbell in the passenger seat, heading south.

Chelsea Ingar's home was located in the heart of town with a front-door view of the devastation left behind by a psychotic ATF agent now serving the remainder of her life behind bars. The sight was a hard reminder of why Battle Mountain had become his new home but failed to drive the photo of his daughter from his mind.

They walked up the cracked sidewalk to a rambler- style home that had seen better days. Bare trees and dying shrubs lined the rectangular yard fenced in with a dilapidated picket fence that all combined to contrast with the Christmas-red front door.

"Probably better if I do the talking. People around here, they're starting to get suspicious of outsiders." Kendric pounded the side of his fist against the door, welcomed by the echo of footsteps on the other side. The door opened inward and revealed a short blonde woman yelling over her shoulder to the three kids rampaging through the house.

"Can I help you?" Blue eyes ping-ponged between Kendric and Campbell, then back again.

"Mrs. Ingar, we're sorry to disturb you. I'm Officer Hudson, Battle Mountain Police, and this is Detective Dwyer. I'm sure you've heard about what happened up the mountain at the Bryon place. We just have a few questions for you, if you're agreeable," he said.

"Not sure how much help I can be." Chelsea glanced over her shoulder, exposing a pattern of dry, angry acne scars down the side of her face. Nervous? "We don't live anywhere near there. We wouldn't have seen or heard anything."

"But you do know Sabrina Bryon, the woman who's gone missing," Campbell said.

Chelsea folded her arms across her midsection. "Only what I've read in the papers. I might've seen her a few times in town. That's all."

Suspicion exploded through him. "Mrs. Ingar, according to phone records, you and Sabrina have exchanged messages every day for the past two years. I'd say that's more than a passing acquaintance."

"I'm sorry, Officer. You're mistaken." Chelsea Ingar stepped back into her house and started to close the door. "I've never met the woman in my life."

"SHE'S HIDING SOMETHING." Campbell could feel it. She replayed the interview through her head. Over and over until every word had been scratched into the surface of her brain. Every syllable. The landscape passed in rushed layers of white snow, melted slurry and thick mud along the street. Gray clouds stitched together in a blanket of darkness and cold and had her wishing for the comfort of the bed she'd woken up in this morning. The one that smelled of Kendric, even though she'd been an entire room away.

The trip to Grand Junction would take most of the day, keeping them from exploring more immediate leads, but given their only witness was finally awake and talking, they couldn't afford to miss this opportunity. Elliot Bryon had been in the house when his wife had gone missing. He was the way to solving this case. "Chelsea Ingar knows where Sabrina Bryon is. She lied to us."

"We don't know that. I told you, the people

of this town are on edge. You have no idea what they've been through the past year." Kendric stared straight through the windshield, green eyes more gray. It was an optical illusion. A minor shift in perspective. One she was frequently reminded of in Penny's eyes when the blue gave way to the same hint of gray on cloudy days. "First a guy burying women in refrigerators, come to find out he was sent here by someone else, then the Contractor, and then Agent Freehan. They're afraid they're next, that one day they'll wake up and BMPD will be on their doorstep telling them someone they love is gone. These people can barely stay afloat during the off season since the mining companies jumped ship. Now we've got a Jane Doe with the coroner, Elliot Bryon has been shot and his wife is missing. Don't tell me Chelsea Ingar doesn't have a right to want to stay away from it all."

"Why Battle Mountain?" She hadn't meant to ask the question that had been nagging her since before she'd taken this case, but it was too late to take it back. Campbell ripped her gaze from the haunting, empty terrain between Battle Mountain and Grand Junction and settled on him. "What do you think it is about this place that draws killers here?"

He didn't answer right away, and her own

law enforcement experience immediately tried to fill in the blanks. Corruption, lies, secrets. Every town—every department and officer—she'd investigated had them, but Campbell couldn't imagine the man sitting beside her getting involved. Not knowingly. "I think it attracts people in need more than killers. I think this town offers something not a whole lot of other places do. Apart from location and access to back roads, it's quiet. Isolated. The people here are friendlier than in the big cities. They've grown up with one another, they're raising their kids together and they like to make an effort to know your name. They're genuine. No tricks. No manipulations. It's simple living at its finest, and they're happy. How many other places can say the same?"

A wistfulness bled from his voice as though he'd experienced all that firsthand. "Is that what attracted you here? The quiet? The community?"

"It wasn't Denver, which was good enough for me." He pressed broad shoulders back into his seat, accentuating fine muscle and tight tendons down the length of his neck. He was handsome. Now more than ever, but weathered and lost. His past had beaten him down, and he hadn't yet found the strength to stand back up. "After everything went down with Agent

Freehan, I took one look at the damage she'd caused and knew Battle Mountain was where I could make a difference. I don't know how to explain it other than that when I got here, something just felt…right. Like I was supposed to be here."

She didn't know what to say to that, what to think. She'd felt that sense of rightness, too. With him. But given how he'd already made his decision concerning building a relationship with her and their daughter, Campbell couldn't see any way to get that back. Not yet. Maybe not ever. She directed her attention back out the window, to the miles of pristine, snow-covered farmland laid out in perfect white sheets. The clouds had descended, spreading out in dark layers and blocking the view of the mountains.

They passed the rest of the trip to Grand Junction in silence. Within the hour, Kendric maneuvered the SUV into the parking lot of St. Mary's Medical Center. Layer upon layer of varying shades of red rock protected the city and allowed the limited afternoon sun to reflect off the one-way glass windows of the towering hospital. Kendric had been right before. It was nothing compared to the beauty and peace she'd felt in Battle Mountain. They moved as one through the building's double glass doors and checked in at the security desk.

Elliot Bryon had been released from the intensive care unit, but considering the circumstances of his need for medical care, visitors were limited to law enforcement and approved family members. Of which he hadn't seen any. Two bullet wounds to the chest created a need for added security measures.

Bright white tile, blinding fluorescent lighting and the scent of bleach in the air were enough to trigger violent memories of her last visit to a hospital like this as she followed Kendric down the hallway.

"Everything okay?" he asked.

Awareness sucker punched her. "Why wouldn't it be?"

"Your breathing changed, and you look like you're about to throw up," he said.

He saw all that? The weight of his attention settled her nerves, somehow talking her down and grounding her at the same time she wanted to jump out of her own skin. Campbell kept her gaze straight ahead and not on the individuals inside the rooms they passed. She tucked her hair behind one ear, hoping for a distraction, but it wasn't enough. "I'm just not a fan of places like this."

Kendric slowed. "Any reason in particular?"

"It doesn't matter." She shook her head, determined to get to Elliot Bryon's room. "I'm good. Promise. My personal feelings about hospitals won't get in the way of what we're doing here."

He reached out to grip one arm, and a shot of heat exploded through her. The effect drowned the hard thump of her pulse behind her ears to the point all she saw, felt and heard was him. "It matters to me."

Her inhalation sawed along her throat. "Penny, uh, stopped breathing during the delivery. She got stuck in the birth canal, and the ob-gyn told me she wasn't going to make it, that there was nothing they could do without risking my life. They were choosing me over her." Campbell slid her hands into her slacks, not ready to meet his gaze. "You can imagine how terrifying that was to someone who hadn't been allowed to eat during twenty-six hours of labor and had no energy to push anymore. I started panicking. I was alone. I didn't know what to do. All these nurses were staring at me with pity and tears in their eyes, and I just… I couldn't take it. I carried her for nine months. It's such a short time, but she was part of me. I didn't want to let her go."

Her eyes burned at the memory.

Kendric drifted his hand higher, sliding his

thumb across her cheek. His jaw had released the tension it had been holding, and easier than she thought possible, she leaned into the strength he offered. "But she survived."

A humorless laugh escaped her control. "I fired the doctor and all those nurses on the spot and demanded another team. The ob-gyn who took over saved her life. Saved both of our lives, but coming here… I'm not a fan."

"I'm sorry you had to go through that alone, that I wasn't there." He motioned to the right side of his face and to the scar tissue that had changed his life, and she was once again reminded of how handsome he was. "Would it help if I told you I'm not a fan, either? This place gives me the heebie-jeebies."

"The heebie-jeebies? Is that a medical term? I've never heard of it until now." Her smile melted at the realization he was still touching her. The heat he'd curated along her arm had transformed into a blister down the length of her jaw and neck. Controlled chaos circled around them, but right then, it was as though they'd created a bubble between them and the outside world. Just the two of them. The hunt for Sabrina Bryon, the investigation into Elliot Bryon's shooting, the identification of Jane Doe—none of it existed inside this moment.

For the first time in years, she felt like she wasn't destined to get through this life alone.

The interruption from the PA system above ripped her back into the moment, and Kendric dropped his hand from her face. "We better get in there. Visiting hours are almost over."

"Yeah." She hung back as Kendric headed for the witness's room. She had to get a hold of herself. He'd made himself perfectly clear on the drive up. He wasn't coming back. He didn't want to be part of her life now as much as the day he'd walked out. And he didn't want a relationship with his daughter. Campbell took a deep breath. Then again, her nerves weren't on high alert anymore. Because of him.

They stepped into the single-bed recovery room. Elliot Bryon lay under the bedding, his face turned away from them. Short dark hair, shorn almost down to the scalp, didn't conceal the receding hairline around a sharp widow's peak. Wide-set eyes turned toward them with a struggle of someone who'd taken two bullets to the chest from close range.

"Mr. Bryon, I'm Officer Hudson from Battle Mountain. This is Detective Dwyer. We'd like to ask you about what happened at your home yesterday morning." Kendric tugged a chair from against the wall beside the bed, then followed up with another. "I understand it may be difficult for you to speak, so please, take your time."

"Did you…find her?" Elliot struggled to form his question despite the help of the oxygen tube. "I already talked to the detectives here. Do you have news?"

"Your wife, Sabrina?" Campbell took her seat closest to the man in the hospital bed. Close enough to count the spouts of gray in his carefully maintained facial hair. A nose that had been broken one too many times angled across a set face, and instantly triggered an ache across her face from last night's antics. She saw no hint of fear, of pain, of nervousness on Elliot's countenance. A blank canvas. "We're doing everything we can. Can you tell us what you remember from the incident? Do you know who shot you and the young woman we found near your home?"

Elliot Bryon nodded. "Sabrina. She tried to kill me."

Chapter Six

"You're saying your wife is the one who shot you and the woman we found dead near your home?" They'd had this all wrong—at least, he had. Campbell had floated this theory, and hell if she hadn't been right. This wasn't a missing persons investigation. This was a manhunt, and Kendric had wasted nearly thirty hours working off the wrong intel. Sabrina Bryon could be anywhere by now. Could have a whole new identity. "You're sure?"

"She found out about me." Elliot Bryon succumbed to a lung-crushing episode of coughs that tensed his shoulders and neck and, Kendric imagined, had landed the man in excruciating pain. He knew the feeling. Their witness relaxed back against the pillows propped behind him, reaching for the glass of water on the side table with shaky hands. "The woman you found... She was a friend."

"You mean you were having an affair." Campbell helped pass off the water.

"Yes." Taking a drink, Elliot Bryon cleared his throat with a lot more color in his face. "I'm not proud of it, but after Sabrina told me she was pregnant, she changed. It was like she was an entirely different person. She wasn't the woman I married."

"What do you mean?" Kendric asked.

"She lost her temper over the smallest things. She just seemed…angry all the time. Distant. She wasn't keeping to her usual schedule and stopped exercising. It didn't matter what I did or if I tried to help, it wasn't good enough. I'm not even sure if she was sleeping," Elliot said. "I'd never seen anything like it. Not with her."

"Pregnancy can affect every woman differently." Campbell's gaze flickered to Kendric, and he was reminded of an entire nine months she'd carried their daughter without his help. And how he never wanted her to go through that again. "Can you think of any reason for her sudden behavioral changes apart from the baby? Were you two planning on starting a family?"

"No." Elliot shook his head. "She made it clear from the beginning, she never wanted kids. Something about her family history. I don't know. I've never met her side. Sabrina was adamant they weren't part of her life, but once she saw that pregnancy test, she was excited. She turned our second bedroom into a nursery the week she found out, not even bothering to wait for the doctor to tell us if we were having a boy or a girl."

"And how did you take the news?" Kendric asked.

"Me?" Elliot's gaze narrowed slightly. His grip tightened on the glass of water in his hand as he moved to set it back on the side table. As though buying himself time to answer. "I come from a big family. I've always wanted a few kids of my own." His expression softened. "If you find Sabrina, if she goes to jail, what's going to happen to the baby? She's due in less than a month. That's my baby. I don't want anything to happen to her."

"Mr. Bryon, we're getting ahead of ourselves. Right now, we just want to bring Sabrina home safely. Any custody issues can be sorted out then." A wrenching twist in his gut reminded Kendric he had his own child to worry about. While Campbell hadn't asked for anything in the way of support for Penny, he had his own obligation to make sure their daughter was taken care of. And he would follow through, even if he couldn't be part of her life. "Can you tell us what happened yester-day morning?"

Elliot Bryon tried to shift his weight in the bed, obvious pain flaring in his face. "Sabrina was supposed to be in town with a friend. They were going to be shopping for the baby all morning, but she came home early. I don't know. Maybe she'd suspected something was going on and lied about where she was going, to see what would happen. All I know is she found me and Rachel together."

"Rachel? The woman you were sleeping with?" Campbell unpocketed a notebook from her blazer, along with a pen, to take notes. "Does Rachel have a last name?"

"Stephenson. Rachel Stephenson." Elliot stared toward the bottom of his bed, a distrac-tion Kendric had become all too familiar with in his own hospital bed for all those months. "We met at work. I run the auto parts store in town. She's one of the parts managers. I mean she... was." He fisted both hands in the hem of his sheets. "She was sweet. She smiled at me. Be-fore I knew it, we were taking our lunch breaks together, telling each other about our lives. I never meant for anything to happen between us. Yesterday... That was the first time we got to-gether. She was so nice, and it just...happened.

I can't believe she's dead. Sabrina never gave her a chance. She just started shooting."

"Do you own a handgun, Mr. Bryon?" Kendric asked.

"Yes. I got it at a gun expo last year." Elliot ran one hand across his chest as though the simple act of talking about the gun that had shot him aggravated the two holes in his sternum. He'd been lucky. One inch to the left, and none of them would be sitting here having this conversation. "Sabrina had just found out about the baby, and she wanted some extra protection. Never thought she'd use the damn thing against me. I thought we were happy."

Obviously not, considering the man had been caught with his pants around his ankles. Kendric caught sight of his partner making another set of notes, her pen nearly going through the notebook. "We didn't recover a weapon at the scene."

"Sabrina must've taken off with it," Elliot said. "I guess I was a little preoccupied with not dying to notice."

"In that case, did Sabrina already have the gun when she came home, or did she go for it during your argument about the affair?" Campbell poised her pen above her notepad.

"I don't… I don't remember." Elliot shook his head, still not meeting their gaze. "Everything happened so fast. I heard her car pull up. I was trying to get Rachel out the back door. Sabrina caught us. She must've already had the gun. She shot Rachel in the back as she was trying to leave. Then she turned the gun on me. I don't remember much after that."

"You don't remember calling 911?" Kendric had listened to that call. Elliot Bryon hadn't said anything about his wife being the shooter, nothing about another victim. Just that he needed medical attention. Kendric had disregarded the lack of information due to extreme panic and the pressure of bleeding out. But his own experience of facing death had him recalling every minute—every second—he'd been trapped in that building after the bomb had gone off.

"No." Another headshake. "Not at all."

"Just a couple more questions, Mr. Bryon, and we'll leave you to rest. You said Sabrina shot you and Rachel by the back door." Campbell tapped her pen against her notebook, and it was then Kendric saw it. The detective on the trail of a possible lead. Her gaze locked onto their witness and refused to let up. Mouth parted, she studied Elliot Bryon with her full attention, and Kendric couldn't help but fear for the man or any other she targeted. "How was it your watch ended up broken in the bedroom?"

Kendric clenched the arm of his chair tighter. The watch she'd collected as evidence from the scene. She was right. Elliot's version of events didn't line up.

"Mr. Bryon?" Campbell asked.

"I remember crawling into the bedroom to hide. That's where the EMTs found me. That's where I must've made the call to 911. I guess it broke then. It's all such a blur." Their witness checked his wrist as though expecting to find the timepiece in place, then rubbed the lighter, watch-shaped skin. "I'm starting to get a little bit light-headed here. Maybe we could cut this short." Elliot Bryon hit the call button for the nurse. "Please. Whatever happens, please don't hurt Sabrina. This is my fault. I did this to us. She's not herself, and I couldn't stand the thought of something happening to her or the baby."

"We'll do our best, sir." Kendric rose to stand. "For now, just focus on getting your rest." He motioned Campbell over the threshold as he closed the door behind them, out of earshot of their witness. "That son of a bitch is lying," he said.

Campbell replaced her notebook in her blazer, turning to face him. Even in this horrible, unnatural lighting, she was a thing of beauty and grace he'd gone too long without appreciating. Strong, independent, capable of upturning his entire world in a twenty-four-hour span. "What gave you that idea? The fact he couldn't make eye contact or that his hand hasn't stopped shaking since we walked into the room?"

"You knew." And he hadn't seen it until a few minutes ago.

"It's my job to spot the signs." Campbell headed down the hallway, not bothering to check if he'd followed after her. "Everything he told us is a lie. If he broke his watch by trying to hide from his wife, who unclasped the band and left it on the floor beside the spot the EMTs found him? Not to mention he went pretty heavy with his wife's behavioral changes due to the pregnancy. Even if we learn Sabrina Bryon is suffering from prenatal depression or is going through some kind of breakdown, it's unlikely she'd turn murderous from hormone changes. Apart from that, it would be extremely difficult for Sabrina to drag the mistress's body into those woods. Something else is going on here."

Kendric strove to keep up with her as they rounded into the corridor leading to the elevators. He hit the descending call button.

"You don't believe me?" she asked.

"The problem is I do." Questioning their only surviving witness was supposed to supply answers into this investigation, but it had done nothing but create new loose ends. "Something he said. That he didn't remember making the 911 call. I listened to that call, same as you, but it doesn't add up. If your wife is the one who shot you, wouldn't that be something you'd mention to police off the bat? Wouldn't you tell them there's another victim?"

Campbell straightened her shoulders. "I guess it depends on the circumstances. I've listened to calls in which someone beaten within an inch of their life remained calm in order to get police all the details they could before they passed out. Others are so out of their minds they can't even hear what the dispatcher is saying. They just want help."

"Exactly, and Elliot Bryon was neither of those things." The elevator signaled its arrival, but Kendric didn't move to step on. Closing the distance between them, he lowered his voice. "I remember every second after that bomb went off, Campbell, and there is not a single day that goes by that I couldn't tell you exactly where I was, where the members of my team were, what time it was, how many seconds were left on the device when I found it, or the last thing I said to you that morning. All of it. Elliot Bryon?" Kendric pointed down the hall. "He can't remember making a call that saved his life? I don't buy it. Because when you're in that position, and your life is on the line, all you can think about is what you've got to lose if you don't make it."

"What are you saying?" Blue eyes scanned him from forehead to chin, and a wake of warmth trailed down his face as though she'd physically touched him.

Kendric couldn't prove it, but he had no doubt in his mind. "I'm saying I think Elliot Bryon made that 911 call before he was shot."

WAS IT POSSIBLE?

Had the surviving witness in their missing persons case been playing his own game from the beginning? Campbell couldn't wrap her head around an answer as she memorized the rise and fall of the mountains out her window. Or as she considered Kendric's words. *When your life is on the line, all you can think about is what you've got to lose if you don't make it.* He'd remembered the last thing he'd said to her that morning. When it had mattered most, one of his last thoughts as he fought for his life had been about her. She'd blocked so much of that time from her mind—to protect herself against the hurt, the confusion, the emotion that came with so much fear when she'd gotten the call— she couldn't remember any of it. "What was it you said to me that morning?"

Kendric adjusted his grip along the steering wheel. "I said I was going to pick up something for dinner on my way home so you didn't have to cook. You'd been especially tired that week. I was trying to be a hero by taking dinner off your shoulders."

"I would've been around eight weeks pregnant at the time. Tired doesn't even begin to describe it." A smile played across her mouth. "She asks about you, you know. Penny. Where her daddy is. Why he's not there. She's already planning her wedding and wondering who's going to walk her down the aisle. I think she's trying to convince me to give her a brother so he can do it."

"What have you told her about me?" His voice caught in his throat. Just enough for her to notice before he cleared the blockage.

"That you're out saving people's lives." She wedged her palm beneath her chin as she visually followed the designs along his face. The slightly puckered, shiny skin hadn't changed much over the years. They were still part of him. Made Kendric who he was despite his hatred for the scars. "That you can't come home until you've saved the entire world. I wasn't too far off, was I?"

"What are you doing, Campbell?" he asked. "Why are you pushing this?"

"Because whether you want to accept it or not, you have a life back in Denver. You have people waiting for you to come home." Couldn't he see that? The man she'd known then wasn't completely gone. There were still pieces of him staring back at her from his eyes when he let down his guard. The Kendric Hudson she'd loved was still in there. "I'm not saying something is going to happen between us again. Maybe there is. Maybe there isn't, but pretending there wasn't anything between us at all—that we don't have a child together—isn't going to make it so."

"I'm not pretending, damn it." The tops of his thighs hardened under the thick layer of jeans. "I know what I gave up. I know the world and all the people in it are moving on without me, and that there's not a damn thing I could do to stop it."

"So why fight?" she asked. "Because you're punishing yourself?"

He didn't answer, didn't even seem to breathe.

"What happened at that conference wasn't your fault, Kendric. What happened to Battle

Mountain wasn't your fault, and these scars are as much a part of you as that thick skull on your shoulders. They don't make you any less of a man or a father to that little girl." Campbell set her hand over his face, against his scars. There was nowhere for him to run. Nowhere to hide here in this small cab of the SUV. "Are you really willing to give up a shot at a family, at being happy, because you refuse to see yourself the way everyone else does?"

"What if she's scared of me?" His words barely registered over the white noise of slushy water and pavement, but they'd struck right through to her heart. His gaze found hers. "What if she won't love me because I look like this?"

A pair of headlights switched to high beams behind them, filling the vehicle and the mirrors with blinding light. It highlighted Kendric's jawline and cast shadows under his eyes.

Campbell removed her hand from his heated face, not really sure how to answer.

His gaze locked on the rearview mirror. He lifted his foot off the accelerator, and the SUV's momentum nudged her forward in her seat. But the pickup refused to go around. Kendric's eyes volleyed between the road ahead and the mirror.

"What are you doing?" she asked.

"This guy won't get off my tail." His knuckles whitened under his grip around the steering wheel.

She spun in her seat, but the brightness of the high beams kept her from seeing through the vehicle's windshield to the driver. Her heart rate picked up. The truck was too close for her to catch the front license plate through the back window. "You think we're being targeted?"

"There's only one way to find out. Tighten your seat belt." Kendric slowed even further, pulling off the side of the road. The belt cut into her shoulder and across her chest as the lights from behind skidded through the cabin of the SUV. The pickup had slammed on the brakes to avoid running into the back of them a split second before Kendric accelerated away from the hood of the second vehicle. Any other driver would've passed by now. Why weren't they?

"I've got a license plate. ADL 211. Colorado. Registration current." The license plate disappeared beneath the bottom edge of the back window. Right before the pickup truck tapped their fender. The jerk thrust Campbell forward, and she gripped the front dash. She grabbed for the radio velcroed to the middle console and hit the push-to-talk-button. "Battle Mountain PD, this is Detective Dwyer, CBI. Officer in need of assistance. Interstate 550. We've got a pickup truck trying to run us off the road. Repeat. Officer in need of assistance. License plate number—"

"Hang on!" Kendric secured an arm across her midsection.

The pickup rammed them a second time.

The radio fell from her hand as the back of their vehicle fishtailed. Kendric tried to keep control of the slide, but freezing temperatures had turned the shoulders of the interstate into an ice rink. Her fingers ached as she braced for impact. "Kendric!"

The back tire caught on something along the road.

Before she had a chance to scream, the fender ripped free of the shoulder and took flight. The hood of their SUV dipped toward the road. Glass shattered from impact and cut across her oversensitive skin. Pain lanced through her temple and across her forehead, but she couldn't distinguish the source. The ground rolled up and over through the windshield as gusts of blistering wind filled the cabin. Metal screeched—too loud—in her ears.

Until there was nothing but silence.

Tendrils of black encroached around the edges of her vision. The lights from the dashboard flickered in and out. Or was that her head playing tricks on her? The high-pitched whine of pavement water and tires filtered through the hard pulse of her heartbeat behind her ears. A vehicle slowing down to help?

Gravity increased its hold on her, the seat belt doing its job keeping her in place, as she realized they'd landed upside down. Snow mixed with broken glass along the ceiling like sparkling diamonds just within reach. That was a weird thought. Searing pain pinched along her forehead, and she managed to bring her hand to the source. Blood crevassed inside of her fingerprints and highlighted the unique loops and whorls. She'd hit her head. She must've sustained a concussion. She had to get out of here. They both did. Blinking to clear the encroaching haze, Campbell stretched her bloodied hand to the driver's side of the vehicle. "Kendric."

No answer.

His face turned away from her, Kendric wasn't moving, and a deep-seated panic took hold. No. No, no, no, no. Her hand shook as she pressed two fingers to the base of his throat. A pulse. He had a pulse. It was unsteady, but it was there. He was still alive. Her lungs released the breath she hadn't realized she'd been holding. "Come on. Wake up. We have to move."

Someone had run them off the road. Targeted them. They couldn't sit here waiting for whoever it had been to finish the job.

Campbell hit the release for her seat belt. Collapsing against the ceiling of the SUV, she moaned as broken glass embedded into the palms of her hands and left shoulder. It didn't matter. She couldn't think about the pain right now.

Footsteps penetrated through the rough exhalations burning up her throat. Movement registered through the back driver's-side window. A pair of boots. Campbell stilled. A Good Samaritan would already be on the phone calling for emergency help. Whoever was on the other side of the vehicle stood stock-still, as though waiting for her and Kendric to make a run for it. Her breath shuddered past her lips as she reached for her sidearm still holstered at her hip.

Cold metal warmed in her hand. One second. Two. She visually followed the boots back toward the other vehicle. A deep growl from the truck's engine vibrated through the frame of the SUV. Relief crashed through her, and Campbell closed her eyes. The driver was leaving.

Setting her weapon against the asphalt now exposed from the broken windshield, she braced one arm against Kendric's shoulder and hit the release for his seat belt. A groan escaped his lacerated throat and mouth.

"I'm going to get you out of here. Okay? Hang on. Help is already on the way." Every muscle in her body protested as she fisted both hands into his jacket and pulled him toward her passenger-side door. There was no telling how much damage he'd sustained until the ambulance and backup arrived, but she would keep him alive. Whatever it took. Her shoulder socket threatened to dislocate as she cleared his body from the vehicle, her instincts on fire. "Why did you have to put on so much…muscle? Why couldn't you consider how it would be for me to drag you across the snow?"

A pinch burned at the base of her neck.

Campbell dropped her hold on Kendric and turned to confront whoever had sneaked up behind her. Too slow. A solid strike across the face thrust her hands first into a foot of snow.

The same pair of boots she'd noted through the SUV's back window penetrated the edge of her vision. "Hello, Detective Dwyer. I think it's time we talked."

She moved to sit back on her heels to get a better look at her attacker, but the world went black.

Chapter Seven

Dying wasn't supposed to be this hard.

Sirens chirped from somewhere off to his right and triggered a splitting headache unlike anything he'd felt before. Kendric forced his eyes open, staring up into a seamless blanket of gray. White flakes drifted from above and melted against his face. What the hell... "Son of a bitch."

Pain lanced through his chest where the seat belt had bruised his sternum and shoulder. Another ache made itself known across his hips as he tried to haul himself up to sit. The red and blue lights blurring at a distance were too bright. Most likely a sign of a concussion or some other kind of head wound. Nothing he hadn't survived before. This time an entire building wasn't threatening to come crashing down at the slightest nudge. Just his pride. "Campbell, you okay?"

He scrubbed both eyes with one hand. No

answer. Snow soaked through his jeans and jacket as he fought to stand. The slam of two car doors triggered a low ringing in his ears. An endless ocean of white stretched out in front of him.

"Kendric?" a familiar voice asked. "What the hell happened?"

He turned, putting two police officers in sight. Both in uniform, armed and looking at him as though he were some kind of caged animal ready to attack. His brain worked to come up with their names, falling short. But he knew them. He recognized their faces. He just couldn't… He pointed at one. "That's a good question, Officer…"

"Ford." Confusion contorted the man's face. Easton's name clicked into place as the former army ranger took a step toward him. "Macie got a request from Detective Dwyer for backup. Said someone was trying to run you off the road. We headed out as soon as we got the call, but it looks like we were too late. You okay, man?"

Ford. Right. He knew that. Recognition supplied the name of the officer at Easton's side. Alma Majors assessed him from head to toe with the darkest brown eyes he'd ever seen, but kept her distance. The Latina archeologist turned reserve officer had been instrumental in taking down Agent Freehan and preventing the rest of Battle Mountain from going up in flames. "Yeah. I must've hit my head. I forgot your name there for a second."

Kendric shook his head. A hulking metal frame demanded attention, and everything inside of him went cold. The flash of high beams, the pickup truck raging at them in the rearview mirror, Campbell's scream as they'd rolled. He forced himself to take a deep breath as the past superimposed over the present.

"Why don't you take a seat, Kendric? You're looking a little out of it." Easton set one hand under Kendric's elbow as Alma took up position on the other side. "The ambulance is two minutes out. Let them give you a once-over before we get your official statement."

"I need to see Campbell," he said. "Where is she?"

"She's not here." Alma pressed her thumb into his forehead to get him to look at her, and a bolt of lightning shot across his vision. And with it another round of pain.

"What do you mean? She was in the passenger seat next to me." He jerked from both of their holds. A good solid foot of snow battled to slow him down, but there wasn't anything that would stop him from getting to Campbell.

"Campbell! She's still in the SUV. She might be injured. Help me. Campbell!"

"Kendric, we already searched the vehicle. There's no one inside." Easton's voice softened as Kendric dived for the passenger-side door. "The seat belt is intact. She wasn't thrown free from the wreckage."

Hinges screamed as he nearly ripped the door free from the frame, exposing Campbell's sidearm inside. No. This didn't make sense. Kendric spun toward the open field splayed out for miles. "She was right here. She wouldn't just leave." There was only one explanation. "Something must've happened. The driver of the pickup. The one who ran us off the road, they must've taken her. She must've dragged me out of the wreckage, and they ambushed her."

"Who?" Alma asked.

Pent-up anger, bitterness and resentment he'd denied all these years erupted. Kendric squeezed his eyes closed and pressed his palms on either side of his head. They'd had the license number of the vehicle. Hell, why couldn't he remember? "I don't know, but it has to have something to do with this case. The missing woman. Sabrina Bryon. We were coming back from interviewing the husband. He's the only surviving witness. Maybe someone didn't want us to bring back information. Maybe Sabrina Bryon isn't who we thought she was. It doesn't matter. I have to find Campbell."

He bolted for the police cruiser. Only when he'd moved to climb behind the wheel, Easton Ford clamped a hand on the driver's-side door.

"Think about this, Hudson. You have no idea where the detective is, if she was taken, who took her or if she's still alive." The war vet refused to budge. "You could be wasting time trying to guess where she was taken, or worse, you could be running straight into a trap. You need to think this through. Come up with a plan before you go off half-cocked."

Kendric didn't have time for this. Neither did Campbell. "Is that what you did for Genevieve when the Contractor had her?" He knew better than to mention Ford's partner. The Alamosa district attorney had barely walked away with her life by the time a serial killer had drilled two screws into each of her knees and left her in a wheelchair. He shifted his attention to the town's rookie officer. "Is that what Cree did for you, Alma? Waited until the time was right? Until he had a plan? Like Agent Freehan was just sitting there waiting for him to come rescue you."

Neither of his fellow officers voiced an answer, and in that silence, he had his own.

"That's what I thought." He ripped the door free from Easton's grip and started the cruiser. Fishtailing away from the wreckage, Kendric kept his eyes forward. Not just on the road but the future. Because no matter how many times he'd tried to tell himself otherwise, Campbell was part of his life. They'd become inextricably linked the moment she'd discovered she was pregnant with their daughter, and faced with the possibility of losing her now, he wasn't ready to give up that connection. "Tell me where you are, Campbell."

He scanned the road, looking for signs of a turnoff, tire tracks—anything that would lead him to her. Campbell was a detective. She was trained to take care of herself, and she knew him inside and out. She'd leave something behind for him to follow. She'd know he'd come for her once he realized she'd been taken. Didn't she?

A wave of dizziness distorted his vision, and the cruiser drifted into the oncoming lane. A horn blared from the other side of the road, and Kendric jerked the wheel back. He had to keep going. He had to find her. He wasn't going to let someone take her from Penny. He wasn't going to lose her again. Squeezing his hands against the steering wheel, he leaned forward to get a better angle of a small disturbance in the snow up ahead. A turnoff? Private property? Hard to tell. The incoming storm would do whatever it took to bury evidence. Whatever it was, he had to take the chance.

Water kicked up alongside the car as he took the turn off the interstate. He hadn't come this far out of town before. There'd been no need while Battle Mountain fought to get back on its feet. Crime, for the most part, had taken a vacation while townspeople tried to recover from the devastation of a forest fire and losing their historic Main Street. Unfamiliar territory stared back at him as he maneuvered the vehicle to a crawl along the unpaved road.

Alma Majors's question echoed on an endless loop. On top of that, why take Campbell at all? Why not him? They'd both been involved in the investigation into Sabrina Bryon's disappearance from the beginning. If the goal had been information, it would've been easier to get access to Battle Mountain's reports through him. Had she been injured to the point the abductor had disregarded her as a threat or just a smaller target, easier to handle? Did that mean Campbell was hurt and needed medical assistance?

He didn't have answers. Right now, they didn't matter. Getting to Campbell. That was all he could focus on. The hood of the cruiser dipped and revolted with the rise and fall of the terrain.

A single structure took shape up ahead, and his pulse rocketed into his throat. A barn that had seen better days and lighter storms stood stark against the backdrop of white-sheet mountains and the colorless expanse of property. He wasn't sure where he was or who this place belonged to. Somewhere between the edge of town and a quarter of the way to Grand Junction. Out of the way. Isolated. Private. The perfect place to bring a hostage.

Kendric shoved the cruiser into Park, careful to keep his distance in case he spooked anyone inside. The best chance he had of making sure Campbell made it out alive was utilizing the element of surprise. He wouldn't fail her. Not again.

Unholstering his sidearm, he released the magazine, counted the number of rounds inside and shoved it back into place. There was no telling what lay beyond the double-wide barn doors, but he wouldn't stop now. Couldn't. For the sake of Campbell's life and for their daughter's.

He shouldered out of the cruiser. His ankles disappeared into a foot of snow. He could already see a fresh set of tire tracks leading up to the barn ahead. He couldn't approach directly.

He'd have to come in from the trees. Heavy flakes threatened to hold him back as he hit the tree line and jogged around the back of the barn. Branches scratched at the skin of his face and neck and caught on his jacket. Numbness had already taken hold in his toes and fingers. Every minute he spent out here was another minute he risked hypothermia. Or worse.

Campbell was worth it.

She was worth everything.

His teeth chattered as he pulled up short of a single weathered door at the back of the structure. Pressing his ear to the splintered panel, he listened for movement—anything that could tell him what waited on the other side. Nothing but silence. "I'm coming, Bell."

Kendric stepped back, raised one leg and targeted the space next to the old lock with his heel. The door burst open wide. He didn't wait for an answering attack and rushed through a thick layer of dust and falling snow. "Campbell!"

He scanned the bare space for signs of life.

The barn was empty.

"Time to wake up, Detective," an unfamiliar voice said.

Water splashed against Campbell's face, shocking her out of a dream she couldn't quite hold on to. Her lungs spasmed for air, and she tipped her head back as her body caught up with her circumstances. She felt heavy, out of it. Dizzy. The back of her neck burned, but the zip ties securing her hands behind her kept her from reaching up and feeling for the source of the pain. "Where am I?"

"Somewhere no one will hear your calls for help." The voice from behind warbled. Not male. Not female. Going from one octave to the next seamlessly as though not quite real. Part of her dream? The distinct sound of a gun slide reached her ears. "I tried to warn you off from searching for Sabrina Bryon with that note and snow globe on your car, but it seems you're as determined as I used to be as an investigator."

"You're... You're a cop." Campbell took in the wood-slatted floor beneath the chair she'd been strapped to, her ankles bound to the chair legs. No give in the zip ties. Nothing to leverage against the plastic to escape. The muscles in her neck failed to hold her head upright, and her chin dropped forward. The drug. Whatever she'd been dosed with hadn't yet worn off, limiting her ability to fight back. "That's how you knew to burn Sabrina's vehicle. How you were able to shoot Elliot Bryon in such a close grouping."

A laugh tendrilled through what looked like an abandoned ranger station. "Not quite. Although it would make sense, wouldn't it? I was put through a vigorous training similar to law enforcement. I just wasn't ever in the business of carrying a badge."

What the hell did that mean? Campbell caught movement through the thick coat of dust of a window just below the roofline of the small structure. A tree? Kendric? Her heart squeezed in her chest. She'd gotten him out of the wreckage after her abductor had run them off the road, but had he survived? "And the woman we found near the Bryon home? Who was she?"

"An unfortunate case of collateral damage." Footsteps registered, and Campbell struggled to bring her head up in time to catch a glimpse of her captor. In vain. "Someone whose life Elliot was willing to risk to get what he wanted, but that's not what I want to talk about right now, Detective Dwyer."

Another pinch at the base of her neck shot searing pain up through her spinal cord and along the synapses in her brain. Her scream echoed off the exposed rafters overhead and shook down through her hands clenched around the chair's arms. She tried to stomp her feet to counter the sensation, but it was no use.

The fire burning through her veins refused to let up, hiking her heart rate into overdrive.

"Now, I'm sure you're familiar with sodium thiopental and its effects on slowing down the messages between your brain and your spinal cord. Crime and forensic dramas love to claim it as some kind of truth serum, but we both know reality doesn't always live up to our hopes." An outline maneuvered in front of her, dragging an identical chair to Campbell's closer. Her abductor took a seat, but trying to get her brain to narrow down specific details triggered another round of dizziness. "I like to use it to get people to focus. See, the best thing about this kind of drug is its ability to keep your brain from straying off topic."

"What do you want?" The question barely escaped her mouth.

"After your visit to Chelsea Ingar's home earlier today, I thought I should get to know you, Detective. The way you think, the way you carry out your investigations. The more I know about you, the better chance I have of making sure you never find Sabrina." The kidnapper's voice dipped another octave, words fusing together and breaking apart over and over until they became clear. "I've read your file. You have a very impressive case history, but none of it tells me why the Colorado

Bureau of Investigations sent you to Battle Mountain to search for Sabrina Bryon. She's a nobody. Not even a blip on your radar. So, what are you really doing here?"

She couldn't. Campbell shook her head as she battled against the drug's effects. Her vision wavered as she tried to memorize the pattern on her abductor's shirt. Red, blue and green plaid, but not flannel. Sweat built in her hairline the harder she tried to keep her story straight. "Tell me what happened to Kendric."

"Not until I get what I want," her kidnapper said.

A lie. Campbell had been through enough interrogations to see the carrot at the end of the stick. Interrogators promised the world for a grain of truth, but she was stronger than this. She wouldn't break. She couldn't. "I…was the most qualified."

"Tsk. Tsk. Tsk." Her abductor leaned forward. Sharp pain exploded at the back of Campbell's head as the kidnapper fisted a handful of hair. Black fabric swam in and out of focus. A ski mask. "I don't want half-truths, Detective. I want the whole story. Why did the CBI send you to Battle Mountain?"

"No." Strain tightened the tendons on either side of her neck. Her fingers tingled from the zip ties cutting off her circulation. She was hot and cold at the same time and wanted nothing more than… "Hot shower, bed. Penny. Kendric."

Had she said that out loud? Campbell squeezed her eyes shut, willing time to rewind, but as her abductor had said, that wasn't how reality worked. Her teeth chattered as the drug took a stronger hold on her nervous system.

The outline in front of her released their hold on her hair, and Campbell fell back against her chair. "Kendric Hudson. Your partner. I didn't realize the two of you were so close. Who's Penny?"

She had to fight. She had to be strong. "My daughter."

Anger festered at the back of her mind. Every word she thought escaped her mouth, a risk she couldn't afford. Keep her mouth shut. That was all she had to do, and she couldn't even do that. "No."

"I see. You're trying to protect her." Her abductor's voice softened. "Is that why you haven't told Battle Mountain PD and your partner that you're with Internal Affairs? I can't imagine they'd want anything to do with you if they knew the truth."

Her gaze snapped to her captor's and triggered a whole new round of dizziness the likes of which she'd never experienced. The world tilted on its axis as her body dragged to one side of the chair. But still she didn't fall. "You don't know what you're...talking about."

"It's obvious now. CBI sent you under the guise of recovering Sabrina Bryon, but your real assignment is to investigate the very people trying to find her. Clever, really. You already had your way into the department's good graces." Her abductor stood, rounding the chair in front of Campbell. "But you're afraid that if the people you've investigated will retaliate, they'll come after your daughter in revenge."

Campbell's darkest fear took control. Her fingernails cut into the base of her palms as the repercussions of her career played out in front of her eyes like they had so many times before. There was an undeniable oath law enforcement officers took upon themselves once they joined the force. Watch each other's backs. Stand together, no matter the cost. Once you were part of it, you were family. That was the deal. But for some, that oath corrupted those looking to put themselves above the law. Convinced them their brothers and sisters in blue would never turn on them or expose them for what they really were. Gave them a sense of immunity.

The men and women she investigated were law enforcement. They had the skills, training and drive to tear her world apart if they discovered the truth. They wouldn't just hurt her for betraying that created family. They'd hurt everyone she ever loved if given the inclination. Her parents. They'd take Penny just to watch Campbell suffer. "Please...she's just a child. Please."

"Don't worry, Detective Dwyer, I'm not here to out you. I have no interest in seeing an innocent child hurt because of the choices of those who are supposed to love them made." The black ski mask was suddenly a few inches from her face. Piercing dark eyes—green at one angle, brown at another—zeroed in on her. A calloused hand squeezed Campbell's chin. "Focus, Detective. This is important. All I want is information about your investigation. You visited Chelsea Ingar's home. You talked to her. What did she say about Sabrina?"

Every inch of her skin tingled. Her exhalations crystallized in front of her mouth. It was so cold. She could hardly curl her fingers. She'd lost the ability to feel her toes. "N-nothing. She claimed she didn't know Sabrina, but the phone records—"

"That's good. What else have you uncovered during your investigation? What is your next move?" the outline asked.

"Move?" The edge of the chair seat bit into the backs of her legs. She blinked to clear the last of the dizziness. The gut-wrenching cry of an infant twisted her head to one side. Had she really heard it? Sodium thiopental wasn't supposed to induce hallucinations but mimic the state of being half-awake and half-asleep. This...this didn't feel right. Something was wrong. "The baby. Where is the baby?"

Her abductor dropped their hand from her face. "What baby?"

"I hear the baby. It's crying. Don't you hear it?" The same way Penny's cries tightened the muscles in her midsection, hearing another child cry initiated a temporary panic that urged her to help. Campbell searched the space, but there was no sign of an infant or that this place was anything more than a cell to be used at her interrogator's whimsy. She wasn't losing her mind. Her voice turned to a whisper. "Don't you hear it?"

"You're reacting to the drug, Detective. There is no baby. There's no one here but you and me." A hard grip on her arm kept her grounded. "Now, tell me what else you know about Sabrina Bryon's disappearance."

Campbell forced her attention from the brown-laced boots she'd memorized at the crash site to the woman standing in front of her. "I know you're her."

Chapter Eight

His gut instinct had led him wrong.

Kendric had searched every damn inch of the abandoned barn. No sign of the truck. No sign of the abductor. No sign of Campbell. He was back at square one and out of time. "Where are you, woman?"

His breath solidified in front of his mouth. The sun had started dipping behind the mountains. While Elliot Bryon's statement didn't sit well, the evidence did. The man who'd claimed his wife had gone off the deep end was stuck in a hospital bed with two bullet wounds in his chest. He hadn't taken Campbell from the wreckage, but could an eight-months-pregnant woman? Despite dropping temperatures, sweat built at his hairline and threatened to throw his body into hypothermia. He had to slow down. He had to think.

Whoever had shot Elliot Bryon—whether Sabrina Bryon or not—was familiar with the area. They'd have to be to stay off BMPD's radar, which meant they wouldn't have chosen a random location to bring a hostage. They'd have done their homework, made sure there was no connection back to the Bryon family. Kendric unpocketed his phone and scrolled to Macie Barclay's number.

The line rang once. Twice. The dispatcher didn't indulge in any pleasantries. "Kendric, I've been trying to get through to you for the past thirty minutes. Easton and Alma said you just took off from the crash site. Do you have any idea—"

"Macie, listen to me." He scanned the barn again, catching sight of a satellite structure through one of the windows. One he hadn't noticed on his drive in. He crouched to get a better view. "Campbell—Detective Dwyer— has been taken, and I need your help."

"Tell me what you've got." The sarcastic, bohemian redhead Kendric found difficult to talk to turned all business.

"Campbell and I visited a woman named Chelsea Ingar earlier this morning. She claimed she doesn't have any connection to Sabrina Bryon, but phone records tell a different story."

"I know Chelsea. Married into one of Battle Mountain's oldest families. Doesn't socialize a whole lot, but I've talked to her a few times at the Baptist church annual picnic. She's always been nice to me, if a little rabbity." Macie lowered her voice as though afraid to get caught up in gossip. "Wait, you think she might be involved in what's going on?"

"I don't know, but it's all I have. I need you to run a property search on the Ingars. Anything out by the interstate." He needed something—anything—to get him closer to Campbell. Kendric backtracked through the door he'd busted past and hiked in thick snow toward the garage-looking structure he'd spotted from the barn. "Anything?"

"Hold your britches, Hudson. It takes a few minutes to break the chief's protocols and run property searches behind his back. But you and I both know I'm going to have to fill him in once he's finished with his midday crash on his keyboard." Distinct taps filtered through the line. "Here we go. Looks like there's a good four acres of land registered to Budd Ingar, Chelsea's husband, not far from your current location."

Kendric pulled up short of the garage and studied the dense line of trees closing in. "How do you know where I'm at?"

"It's not because I put a tracker in your

bootheel when you weren't looking," she said. "I'd never do that."

He kicked up his back heel. It was a joke. The dispatcher never would've had access to his boots. Except those first couple of weeks he'd stayed at Whispering Pines Ranch/temporary Battle Mountain PD station while the old station was brought back to life. No. She wouldn't have. He would've noticed. "Where's the property?"

"Keep heading west. You're practically on the border. Kendric, in all seriousness, be careful. The Ingars aren't known for hospitality—" The phone cut out.

Kendric closed in on the dilapidated structure ahead. Tire tracks disappeared under the beaten and weathered garage door. Fresh. Not more than an hour old if he had to guess. The edges of the imprints were still razor-thin. No hint of erosion. He crouched, wrenching the heavy door above his head. And exposed a pickup with a dented fender parked inside. An echo of Campbell's voice raced through his head. *ADL 211.* This was the truck. The one that had run them off the road. He set his hand over the hood. Still warm. "You couldn't have gotten that far."

Unholstering his weapon, he rounded to the driver's side of the vehicle and pried open the door. Warm air escaped the cabin as he studied the interior. A hint of bleach tickled the back of his throat. Hell. The entire inside had been wiped down. Steering wheel, dashboard, even the leather seats. No chance for prints or DNA, but considering how far Sabrina Bryon had gone to cover her tracks, he shouldn't have expected any less. Pulling himself inside, Kendric went for the glove box and tugged the vehicle's registration free. "Ingar."

Made sense. The truck was being stored on land registered to the same owners, but were they aware of what someone had done in their name?

"You're going to want to get of out my husband's truck real slow." The feminine voice barely registered over the cocking of a shotgun held in the hands of a woman too small to shoulder it correctly. One pull of that trigger and Chelsea Ingar would find herself in a world of pain. "Now."

Guess that answered his question. Kendric raised his hands in surrender, the truck registration still in one hand, as he slid from the driver's seat. His weapon stared back at him from the leather seat, but he only had attention for the five-foot woman who'd caught him with his hands in the cookie jar. "Chelsea, good to see you again."

"This is private property. Battle Mountain PD has no right to step foot on this land without my permission, and I sure as hell don't remember giving you permission when you came to my house this morning." Chelsea Ingar's nervous gaze darted from Kendric to the truck and back. This wasn't the spitfire mother of three he'd met this morning. No. This was a woman on the edge. Afraid he'd found something inside?

Kendric stayed within arm's reach of his sidearm. Although, he hoped to hell and back he wouldn't have to use it. "Oh, good. You do remember me. Then you'll also remember the woman I was with. Detective Dwyer. She's gone missing."

"What does that have to do with me?" Chelsea adjusted her grip on the shotgun.

"Maybe nothing," he said. "Maybe everything. You lied to us this morning when you said you didn't know Sabrina Bryon. You've been in contact with her. You've been helping her. Now, I'm not sure how much she's told you about what happened with her husband and his mistress, but I can guarantee you're helping her with faulty information. Someone used this truck to run me and my partner off the interstate about an hour ago, and now my partner is missing."

"It wasn't supposed to be like this," she said.

"I can understand you're a woman lodged between a rock and a hard place. You want to do what's best for your friend. You're trying to help, but Sabrina Bryon isn't who you think she is, Chelsea." Kendric angled himself behind the driver's-side door. "Do yourself a favor. Put down the gun. Think about those kids you've got back home. Think about Budd. What shooting me will do to your family."

A humorless laugh escaped the woman's throat, and suddenly the woman's nerves weren't what Kendric was most worried about. "You want me to think about Budd? No, Officer Hudson. You don't want me to think about my husband with his shotgun in my hands. Not unless you won't miss your organs." Chelsea Ingar shifted her weight between both feet. "You want to know how Sabrina and I met? In the clinic in town. She was there to get a checkup on the baby while I was there to see if the one I had was still alive after my husband was finished with me. She was nice. She listened to me. She held me while I cried right there in the middle of the damn waiting room. No one had ever done that for me. My family doesn't believe me when I tell them what a monster he's been since he lost his job in the mines, and his family only reminded me that's the cost of marrying an Ingar. Sabrina was the only one who cared, the only one who was just as angry as I was. Do you really think I was going to turn my back on her when she needed my help?"

"So you lent her Budd's pickup, told her about the property out here to give her a place to hide until she could get out of town," he said. "If anyone came asking, you were to deny you knew each other. Did she tell you what happened with her husband?"

"She didn't have to tell me." The weight of the shotgun exhausted Chelsea's arms, and the barrel dipped lower. "I could see it on her face when she showed up on my doorstep after Budd had left for the liquor store. I could see the blood on her clothes. I didn't ask questions. I just handed her the keys to the truck and this address."

Kendric slipped his hand along the driver's-side door, closer to his sidearm. "You wanted to help her same as she helped you. I can appreciate that. Truth is, I'm in the same kind of position with my partner. You see these scars?" He motioned to the right side of his face. "I spent eight weeks in the hospital burn unit recovering after a bomb blew up in my face. Every time I woke up, no matter what time of day, she was there. When I look back, I realize she's the reason I pulled through, of why I'm standing here today. Now, all I want to do is help her, but I can't do that without you, Chelsea. I need you to tell me where Sabrina is keeping her."

"I don't know." Chelsea shook her head. "I haven't heard from her since yesterday morning. I waited until Budd passed out, dropped the kids off with my neighbor and came up to check on her."

"All right, then. I believe you. So, what are you going to do now?" His heart rate kicked into overdrive as his gaze lowered to the end of her shotgun staring right at him. "Are you going to kill an unarmed man, a Battle Mountain police officer, for Sabrina? Are you going to let her kill my partner? She has a daughter, too. A four-year-old. Are you going to leave her little girl without a mother?"

Her eyes watered with unshed tears as Chelsea positioned her index finger over the trigger. "You weren't supposed to be here. Neither of you were."

He wasn't getting through to her.

"Chelsea, listen, I can help you. I can make sure you and your kids walk away from this. I can make sure you get away from Budd. We can forget it ever happened." Kendric slipped his hand around his weapon, heart in his throat, as the seconds ticked by. "But you need to hand me the shotgun."

"I'm sorry, Officer Hudson." Chelsea took aim. "I can't do that."

A gunshot exploded through the garage.

A GUNSHOT.

Campbell heard it clear as day. It had been close. Within at least a quarter of a mile. Someone was out there. Someone was coming. Kendric? Her chest tightened as she considered the danger he'd walk into by coming after her, countered by the hope he had.

The watery outline of her captor in front of her twisted toward a single window on the opposite wall of the ranger station.

The drug was still messing with her senses, but they were getting clearer every second. She just had to focus. Campbell swung her left elbow out wide to twist the zip tie securing her to the chair. "You have no idea what you've done, do you? What kind of hell you're bringing down on yourself? Save yourself the trouble and let me go. You don't want to face what's on the other side of that door."

"You're trying to scare me, to get me to react irrationally, but I promise, Detective Dwyer, I'm thinking clearer than I have in years." A femininity tinted her abductor's words, then faded, verifying Campbell's theory. Sabrina Bryon had run them off the road. She'd drugged Campbell, brought her here to interrogate her about the investigation, but the woman's shape wasn't that of an expecting mother. Not entirely.

Campbell caught herself in the middle of the thought. That didn't make sense. Were the drugs still altering her perception, or had Sabrina Bryon been lying about the pregnancy all along? She recalled the pregnancy pillow discovered with Jane Doc—now Rachel Stephenson—in the woods near the primary crime scene.

Sabrina withdrew a weapon Campbell hadn't noted from the small of her back and turned to face her hostage. "No one is coming for you. Not until I get what I want."

"I've answered all of your questions. You made sure of that." Closing her eyes, Campbell fought to regain control of her own body, but the drug, coupled with dropping temperatures, had stolen every last ounce of her defenses. "I don't have anything else to say to you."

"Sure, you do." Sabrina Bryon slipped the ski mask from her face. A tumble of curly auburn hair staticked against the fabric. Wide brown eyes targeted Campbell as her abductor took her seat again, but the woman smiling out from the photos in the Bryon home didn't compare to the real version. Smooth skin unmarked by scars or age, straight white teeth. "While I have the training and skills to carry out an investigation of my own, you can appreciate how limited I am considering the police have posted officers guarding my husband's hospital room."

Campbell couldn't hold back her disbelief, and a scoff escaped her fraying control. "So that's what this is about. Your husband. Why lie about the baby?"

Surprise countered the hard set of Sabrina's mouth. "Who said I was lying?"

"We found a pregnancy pillow at the scene, and you're obviously not eight months pregnant." Campbell's gaze drifted down the length of her abductor's body without her consent, her attention locking on a darker stain near the woman's breast. "Why convince your husband and everyone in town you're expecting? To what end?"

Sabrina sat back in her chair, the gun laid across her lap. "You really have no idea who or what you're investigating, do you, Detective? I wasn't lying. I was pregnant."

"But you're not anymore." Her gut clenched. She'd thought she'd imagined it. The cry of an infant nearby. Campbell took in the bareness of the ranger station, the dust, the growth of weeds long dead through the floor slats. "You had the baby."

Her abductor leaned forward. "Let me guess. Elliot told you I was the one who shot him. That I'm the one who went off the deep end when I found out I was pregnant. Do you believe him?"

Campbell didn't know what to say, what to think. Sabrina Bryon had been forced to give birth in this place, without support, without a medical team to make sure nothing went wrong. How? How had she done it? Why did it matter? There'd been a gunshot not far from here. If Kendric had been on the receiving end, he was running out of time. She had to get out of here. She had to get to him. Campbell lowered her voice and dropped her head, succumbing to the drug entirely. "It doesn't matter what I believe. I follow the evidence."

"And what is the evidence telling you, Detective?" Sabrina got even closer, burying the gun in her lap.

"That you're out of time." Campbell brought her head up fast. The back of her skull connected with Sabrina's chin. The zip tie around her left wrist snapped with added effort, and she shoved her abductor away.

Sabrina and her chair tipped backward.

The gun fell from her abductor's grip and slid across the floor as Campbell pulled her right wrist free. Only she wasn't fast enough. A hard right hook slammed into her face as Sabrina got her footing. The floor rose to meet her as she collapsed from her ankles still tied to the chair's legs. Her fingers brushed the grip of the gun a split second before a bootheel slammed down on the back of her hand. Bones crunched beneath the weight, and Campbell's scream filled the station.

Another round of crying pierced her ears as Sabrina collected the weapon from the floor and took aim. "Hasn't anyone ever told you not to wake a sleeping baby?"

Campbell twisted onto her back as much as she could with her ankles still attached to the chair. "You don't want to do this."

"I thought you and I could be friends, Detective." Sabrina pulled the slide of the weapon back and loaded a bullet into the chamber. "But you're just like him, aren't you? A fraud."

The door of the station slammed back against the wall. A distinct outline filled the frame. "Put down the gun. Now." Kendric stood there with his weapon aimed, every ounce the police officer she'd imagined him to be. Justified. Strong. Rational. Everything she'd needed right then. "Sabrina Bryon, you are wanted for questioning in the shooting of Elliot Bryon and Rachel Stephenson, as well as vehicular assault and the abduction of a law enforcement officer."

"Officer Hudson, glad you could join us, and bullet-free and healthy, from what I can see." Sabrina kept cold eyes on Campbell. Full lips flattened, and for a moment, Campbell could've sworn there was real regret in those dark eyes. "I take it Chelsea is dead?"

"No, but she's not going to be using her right arm anytime soon." Kendric crossed the threshold. "Drop the weapon, get on your knees and put your hands over your head. Refuse and you and Chelsea Ingar can have side-by-side hospital beds, complete with your own set of matching cuffs."

"Kendric, the baby." Campbell fought to control her breathing as her memories of her own child flashed at the back of her mind. Penny. The dark stain on Sabrina's shirt had doubled in size. Breast milk. The woman had gone on the run eight months pregnant and become a mother in less than twenty-four hours. "Her baby is here. She delivered a month early. We need an ambulance."

"She's not going anywhere with you." Sabrina arced her weapon up, taking aim at Kendric. "And neither am I."

"No!" Campbell lunged off the floor.

The gun discharged before she managed to wrap both arms around Sabrina's legs. Her abductor fell back, another shot exploding close to Campbell's head. The sound had punctured her ears—too close in such a small space—but it was the heavy drop of a body that forced ice through her veins. They hit the floor as one in a tangle of limbs and survival. Her damn ankles were still bound to the chair, but she had enough movement in her upper body to wrestle the gun away and pin Sabrina Bryon to the floor. Until Campbell caught sight of her partner.

"Kendric." His name tore from her lips. Panic infused along her muscles as the world came to a crashing halt. She'd come to Battle Mountain on her own agenda. A few days ago, all Campbell had wanted was to find the source of the problems in the small sleepy mining town on the verge of collapse. Now all she could think about was what she'd lose if she left. "What did you do?"

A hard strike rocketed white lightning across her vision. "What I had to."

Campbell fell back, and she hit the floor a second time. The bite of hardwood didn't take the sting out of her face or the grief charging up her throat as she studied Kendric's still frame.

Sabrina Bryon shot to her feet.

Reverberations of footsteps rumbled beneath her as Campbell shoved herself off the floor. Twisting one ankle at a time, she broke the zip ties securing her to the chair just as her abductor leveled her weapon at Campbell's chest.

"I gave you a chance, Detective, but if you're not with me, you're against me, and I will do whatever it takes to win." The new mother clutched a still, blanket-wrapped package to her shoulder from a closet on the other side of the room. The baby. It wasn't crying anymore, and Campbell's heart hurt at the possibility dropping temperatures had triggered the infant's body to start shutting down. "If you want to make it back to your daughter, do yourself a favor. Don't follow me."

Sabrina Bryon disappeared out the opposite entrance to the ranger station. Every cell in her body wanted to chase after the woman responsible for the shooting of three people, but she couldn't leave Kendric to bleed out.

"Kendric." Campbell raced to his side. Blood spread from a shoulder wound—too much blood—and she set both palms over the hole to contain the flow. She wasn't a field medic. She didn't know a damn thing about patching bullet wounds. "Don't you dare give up now. You hear me? Hang on."

Keeping pressure on the wound with one hand, she searched his person. She needed a radio or a cell phone. Some way to contact his department. For the second time in less than two hours, Kendric's life had been left in her hands.

And she wasn't going to let him go.

Chapter Nine

He'd come to Battle Mountain to escape the pain. Not make it his best friend.

A groan worked up Kendric's throat as he tried to roll off the arm that had fallen asleep. Another explosion of pain ricocheted across his back and down his arm. Not asleep. Oh, hell.

"You're awake." That voice. Her voice. It charged along his nerve endings and released the tension building down his spine. Campbell. He wasn't sure he'd ever hear that sweet sound again. "Take it easy. The EMT just got the bullet out."

Bullet? The past rushed to meet the present and filled in the missing holes in his memory. The crash. His race to find Campbell alive. Sabrina Bryon pulling the trigger. Warmth radiated from his right side, beading sweat at his temple. The last thing he remembered was a never-ending coldness dripping through him like an IV. Kendric rotated his wrist, flaring another round of pain. Wait. That was an IV, but this didn't feel like a hospital. Too warm. Too quiet. Dryness caked the inside of his mouth as he pried his eyelids open. Dark wood lined the ceiling and highlighted exposed rafters. The heat trying to sweat him dry was coming from a fireplace nearby. Flannel pillows, animal skins, the head of a deer mounted on the opposite wall—he certainly wasn't in Kansas anymore. "Where am I?"

"You're safe." She brushed his hair away from his forehead, staring down at him with those cerulean blue eyes he'd dreamed of so many times. Hair pulled back to expose the length of her neck and full shape of her face, Campbell had changed out of her pantsuit armor and into a white T-shirt and jeans that emphasized the bruises and cuts along one side of her face and down her arms. "You told me how much you hated hospitals. I figured you would recover easier someplace you already know. Your chief brought in an EMT to take care of the wound."

"Just in time, too. Another few minutes, and you might've bled out right there in the middle of the woods." Another outline penetrated his vision. Cold metal from a stethoscope slipped across his chest and stole a hiss from between his teeth. An elfin-thin face and wide brown eyes solidified above him as short brown hair dislodged from behind the woman's ear. Isla Vach—one of Battle Mountain fire and rescue's EMTs—stretched her mouth into a thin, compassionate line. "Sorry. I always forget to warm these things up. Vitals are stable. Should be good as new in a few weeks. Just try to take it easy until then. Got it?"

"Thank you." Campbell stood to shake the tech's hand across his bed. "For everything."

A wrap of white bandaging encircled the hand at her side. Coupled with the butterfly closure across her forehead, she obviously hadn't gotten out of this as unscathed as he'd hoped.

"Always happy to help." The EMT flashed another weak smile as she packed her supplies and hauled her duffel bag over one shoulder. "Now, if you don't mind, a certain six-year-old is waiting for me to come home and read her a book for the thousandth time today. Glad you're okay, Hudson. Not sure we could afford to lose you with all this excitement going on." Isla didn't wait for them to answer, heading for the cabin's door.

Recognition permeated through the haze threatening to pull him back into unconsciousness. He'd visited Whispering Pines Ranch enough times to place the cozy cabin decor usually reserved for big city tourists looking for a bit of ranch life. The proprietor and owner, Karie Ford, had taken over running the place since her husband had been murdered by a serial killer going after Battle Mountain's very own coroner, Dr. Chloe Pascale. It was on this land her son Easton Ford had built his veteran rehabilitation center after his fiancée had lost the use of both legs. Recently, though, it had served as a police headquarters while the engineers tried to piece the original station back together.

"How long was I out?" Sandpaper lodged in his throat.

"Two days." Campbell trailed her thumb along the back of his hand while his two lives intersected. One after a bomb had tried to rip him apart and one where he'd believed he could actually make a difference in a small town on the brink of destruction. Funny how Campbell had been such a big part of both. "The bullet nicked your brachial artery. Isla didn't want to risk you tearing your sutures, so she gave you something to sleep to get over the first hurdle of recovery."

"And Sabrina?" he asked.

"Gone. I didn't… I didn't want to leave you to chase after her." A hint of regret cast her gaze down where she'd interlaced her fingers with his. She'd wanted to catch Sabrina, to be the one to solve this case, and he'd just been dead weight. An obligation. Same as before. "Your officers—Easton and Alma—found Chelsea Ingar in cuffs in the cruiser. They took her into custody, got the graze on her arm patched up and have filed charges with a condition that if she gives up Sabrina Bryon, they'll drop them. So far she hasn't said anything."

"She won't talk." Unwinding his fingers from hers, Kendric struggled to sit up, forgetting all about the hole in his shoulder. Another groan tore from his throat, and Campbell moved in to help.

"You shouldn't try to move," she said. "You could start bleeding again."

"I'm fine." The words left his mouth harsher than he'd intended, but it was nothing compared to the resentment bubbling to the surface. Who had he been kidding? How the hell did he expect his new life to be any different than the old one? People didn't change. He didn't change, and he wouldn't be the reason this case failed. Kendric inched his weight to the edge of the bed and sat up, one hand slapped over the thick pads of gauze on his wound. "I know you'd rather be out there looking for Sabrina Bryon. Go. I can take care of myself."

"Chief Ford and Gregson are combing through the scene to get a lead on where Sabrina might've gone. Officer Majors is with Chelsea Ingar. Given their shared…history, I thought it best for her to take point during the interrogation." She lowered her voice, carrying far more respect for Battle Mountain PD's newest recruit than he expected. While Alma Majors's history with domestic abuse wasn't public knowledge, Campbell had made a good call. "Sabrina can't get far. She has an infant with her now. She has to think about them both, which will slow her down. The only thing I'm concerned about right now is you."

"Like I said, I can take care of myself." He needed a shower, a clean set of clothes and anything Karie Ford had lying around the kitchen. Kendric moved to stand, but his body had yet to catch up with the order. He tipped forward. He automatically commanded his wounded arm to catch his fall, and a gut-wrenching pain lanced down his back.

Campbell caught him before he face-planted in front of her. Hauling him against her hip, she angled him back down onto the edge of the mattress. "Right, and may I say, you're doing a fantastic job."

Damn it. Whatever sedative Isla had given him had wreaked havoc on his nervous system. He wasn't going anywhere anytime soon. Settled back onto the bed, Kendric forced himself to not look at her. He didn't want to see the pity there. He couldn't do this again. "Just like old times."

"Except this time, we're not separated by a hyperbaric chamber." She swiped her uninjured palm down her jean-clad thigh. "And you've still got your good looks."

Kendric's control slipped, and he raised his gaze to hers. Only there wasn't pity in her expression as he'd judged. It was something else. Something along the lines of…admiration. How was that possible? He hadn't done anything back at that ranger station but make the situation more complicated, and here she was looking back at him as though he'd saved the day. "How do you do it? How can you sit there pretending I don't look like this? Like I'm still the man you knew all those years ago?"

"Because you are the same man to me." Campbell shrugged as though she hadn't just rocked his entire world. As though her answer was the most obvious thing in the world. "No amount of circumstance or scars is going to change that. You tore through those woods looking for me the same way you tore through that building looking for civilians. I'm able to sit here without a bullet of my own because you charged into that room no matter what was waiting on the other side, same as you charged into that conference before the bomb went off. I can go back to our daughter in one piece after this case is closed, and I will always be grateful for that."

She raised her hand to his face, slowly, cautiously. "You keep telling me the man I loved all those years ago doesn't exist, but I still see him in your eyes. I felt him when you kissed me."

He braced himself for the fear and contempt that always followed physical contact, but she felt so good. Grounding and exhilarating at the same time. Warm and reliable. Perfect. "Campbell…"

"I see the idealistic, passionate, protective man I asked out for a date in the middle of that crime scene." She scanned his face from forehead to chin, and in that moment, he'd never felt more exposed. Or more trusting. "Nothing has changed for me."

Her words drilled past his defenses and tore down the self-hatred he'd been thriving on for years. She couldn't have meant what had come to mind. Not after all this time. Not after everything he'd done. "Nothing?"

"Nothing." Her wide smile flashed bright, and Campbell kissed him.

Soft lips glided against his. The action rocked him straight to his core. Every cell in his body ignited with each stroke of her tongue, and there wasn't a single part of him that could fight it. He'd convinced himself kissing her in his kitchen a few days ago had been a fluke, something that couldn't be replicated. In a way, he was right. This was nothing like that first kiss between them. In that moment, he'd never experienced anything more intense, more satisfying, and hell, it turned him inside out faster than before.

Kendric pulled her against him, immediately regretting the strain on his arm. He ended the kiss, but he was far from finished tasting her. Coming out of his wince, he opened one eye in a flood of embarrassment. "I forgot about the arm."

"It might take some getting used to," she said. "For both of us."

"Worth it." He crushed his mouth to hers.

CAMPBELL MANEUVERED OUT from under Kendric's arm and slid free from the bed.

He'd fallen asleep mere minutes after kissing her, and she couldn't blame him. The bullet had nearly killed him. Beating death once from that bombing—let alone twice—was a process. One he couldn't push through or skip steps.

The fire had died to low embers, and she set another log from the pile off to one side on top to get the heat back up. Whispering Pines Ranch was unlike anything she'd experienced before. The owner, Karie, had fed her and the entire Battle Mountain PD uncomplainingly, with warming, filling foods Campbell hadn't indulged in since she'd been a kid. Fluffy waffles, handmade hash browns, perfect eggs, sugary syrup. And that had just been for breakfast. Her parents had always ensured she hadn't gone hungry when she was growing up, but Karie Ford had no trouble making sure Campbell couldn't squeeze in another bite. And then some.

She studied the man unconscious on the bed as the new log caught fire.

This place… It felt different than Denver. Different than the CBI. Like there was a warmth she couldn't quite define. She'd listened to Easton and Weston Ford bicker and banter since the moment she'd stepped foot on the land. During the large mealtimes around the old hand-carved table for twelve. During chores around the main cabin and on the property. Even while the brothers worked to protect the town they obviously loved. Only it wasn't just them but Cree Gregson, too, a man she'd known from her former days in the sheriff's department. All of them took cheap shots with wide smiles, and when it came to the women in their lives—their mother, their partner, their fiancée, their dispatcher and the mother of their child—the connection carried through. The men and women serving this town had a bond unlike anything she'd seen in Denver, even when she'd been in the midst of it. And for the first time since she'd taken this case, she saw what Kendric saw here. A family.

These people had obviously welcomed him as one of their own. They cared. They worried and hovered like overprotective siblings. They had his back, which was more than she could say in her current position in Internal Affairs. For the officers who knew where her loyalties lay, she'd become a pariah. Someone to avoid, to fear. Every word had to be calculated, every question answered just so, so as not to raise her suspicions. She'd become an outsider in her own department when what she'd really wanted, what she'd needed, was…this. A family of her own.

But every family had secrets.

And what she and Penny had was perfect. They were happy. They were enough.

Campbell donned the pair of boots Genevieve Alexander—Easton Ford's fiancée and the district attorney of Alamosa, CO—had lent her to replace her mud-caked heels after the showdown with Sabrina Bryon. With a final glimpse to make sure Kendric was still asleep, she gathered her coat from the hook on the wall and escaped out into the night, closing the door softly behind her.

Six satellite cabins surrounded the main house. Chief Ford and Dr. Pascale in one, Cree Gregson and his partner, Alma, in another, Kendric and Campbell in the third and Easton and Genevieve in a fourth. The fifth cabin had been left empty for any tourists wanting to brave the desolate Colorado winters here in the mountains, and the sixth held the answers she needed.

Snow twinkled and crunched under her feet as she cut along the main cabin. The drift of laughter reached her ears across the barren landscape, and Campbell slowed. Lights from inside the nearest satellite cabin high-lighted Cree Gregson and Alma Majors locked in an awkward dance around a small kitchen table. Both still wore their uniforms with wide smiles plastered on their faces, and before she had a chance to realize what she'd done, she'd stepped closer to get a better view.

They looked happy. In love. The way Cree

stared down at his partner lodged in her mind until Kendric's face superimposed over the scene. They'd had that once upon a time. That kind of…bliss. It had been short and fleeting considering the time they'd been together, but that hadn't made it any less real or monumental. Would he ever look at her that way again? Could he after everything he'd been through? It didn't matter. Even if he'd managed to overcome his own self-loathing, she'd lied to him since the moment she'd stepped onto that crime scene four days ago. While they'd had a full and rich relationship—one that had resulted in the most beautiful little girl—they weren't compatible now. Not as long as she led the investigation into his department. Not as long as she couldn't be honest with him.

"You're out late, Detective." Chief Weston Ford left the shadows of the main house. He tossed a toothpick into the bushes lining his mother's cabin and swept his jacket back away from his weapon for another in his pocket. "Can't sleep?"

Campbell swiped at her face, only then realizing how close she'd come to blowing her cover. Had he been watching her the entire time? "Something like that. I didn't realize anyone else was still awake. Hope I didn't bother you." From the look of him fully dressed and armed, she hadn't.

"You'd think I'd sleep like a rock with the baby being up every couple of hours, but once I'm up, I'm up. Chloe, though, I don't think a marching band could disturb her," he said.

She didn't miss those days. "Wait until he can scream your name. That'll really get your blood pumping in the middle of the night."

"I didn't realize you had children." Chief Ford bit down on the second toothpick. "Actually, I don't really know anything about you other than what Kendric has told us. You both worked for the Loveland sheriff's department before you made your way to CBI in Denver. Got a pretty good case history in missing persons under your belt. More cases closed than any of your peers. Your file doesn't say a whole lot more than that. Although, I've gotta say, it's impressive."

He'd looked into her. Of course he had. Anyone in his position would've done the same, but what was the point in telling her now? "I'm sorry I haven't had much opportunity to debrief you myself. It wasn't my intention to leave you out of my assignment. In missing persons cases, the faster I can get my feet on the ground, the better."

"Hey, I understand. When CBI sends their

best investigator to help recover a missing young mother in my town, I'm not going to fight it. Anything we can do to bring her home." The chief closed in on her, completely at home with the dropping temperatures and surroundings. "What I don't understand is why you're still here."

Her instincts prickled warning. "What do you mean?"

"I mean this isn't a missing persons case anymore. This is a manhunt. We've got testimony from a witness point-blank accusing Sabrina Bryon of shooting him. Kendric gave a statement she's responsible for running the both of you off the interstate, and you were abducted by the woman for information. When we catch her, and we will, she'll be arrested for murder, attempted murder and anything else I can charge her with." Weston Ford tipped his ten-gallon hat back, exposing deep lines across his forehead. "So that leaves me wondering, why are you still here?"

Her mind instantly went to the sixth satellite cabin, but Campbell held his gaze so as not to give away anything that might compromise her assignment. Battle Mountain had gone forty years without a single homicide, but within months of Weston Ford taking the helm, there'd been two serial killers, a spree killer and a rogue ATF agent ripping through this town. She should be the last concern on his mind. "Kendric was shot. I wasn't just going to leave him."

He stared at her as though trying to see into her mind, but Campbell had perfected the art of compartmentalizing a long time ago. It was a skill that had saved her life more than once in the line of duty. His gaze flickered toward the cabin she'd targeted, before getting caught up in the couple through the window, then back to her. "You should get some rest, Detective Dwyer. If this case leads where I think it will, you and Kendric are going to need it."

He maneuvered past her, putting at least another two feet between them as he headed for the sixth cabin housing Battle Mountain PD's temporary headquarters.

She spun to meet him. "You're not taking him off the case?"

"Couldn't even if I wanted to." Chief Ford kept walking. "The man is more stubborn than he knows what's good for him. Good night, Detective."

"Good night." She watched the chief unlock the satellite cabin door and disappear into the darkness on the other side. A moment later, light filled the cracks around the covered windows. She buried her hands in her coat and retraced her steps. So much for making headway tonight. Shoving through the door to her and Kendric's cabin, she peeled out of her boots and jacket as quietly as she could, so as to not wake him.

"You're back." Gravel laced his voice and triggered a wave of goose bumps down her arms. "Good to see you haven't changed your mind."

"Just went for a walk. Ran into your chief along the way." Despite the warmth of the fire and being in such close quarters, the chill in her bones refused to abate. Had Chief Ford suspected why she'd been out tonight? Would he tell Kendric the first chance he got? Campbell slid onto the edge of the mattress, right where she needed to be. "He told me he wasn't in the business of taking his officers off their cases, even with fresh bullet wounds."

"He knows I won't back down. Not until we find Sabrina Bryon." He ran his uninjured hand along her forearm. "You're freezing."

"Not sure you know this, but it's snowing outside. That usually only happens around the freezing point." She couldn't fight the smile on her lips as she studied him. It was easy to imagine him swinging her around the kitchen, just as she'd seen Cree Gregson and Alma Majors dancing in their cabin, unaware of her attention. Easy to imagine them cozying on a couch for family movie night, his hand laid over the back of hers across the couch as Penny sat between them. Of him taking her to bed each night and waking with satisfaction every morning, of vacations and runs to the grocery store. Of being in love. All the things a family was supposed to be. Her smile faded. Those fantasies were of another life, one in which Kendric wanted to be a father and a partner and where she wasn't lying to him every second she kept a part of herself hidden. Fantasies wouldn't do either of them a bit of good.

For now, they just had to accept reality and make every moment count before they moved on with their lives. She back in Denver with Penny. He here, serving and protecting the people of this town. Her heart pinched in her chest as grief flared hot over her skin. She'd lose him again. Only this time, she wouldn't be alone.

Kendric dragged her beneath the covers, fully clothed, until she pressed against him from shoulder to toes. His heart beat steady under her hand, strong. He kissed her temple, then cuddled closer. "I think I can help warm you up."

That was what she was afraid of.

Chapter Ten

The constant reminder of something he couldn't ever have was painful.

Kendric peeled his cheek from the crown of Campbell's head. The haze of sleep had taken them both harder and faster than he'd expected. His shoulder screamed for relief as the muscles around the bullet wound stretched and relaxed at his instruction, but he wouldn't wake her. Not yet.

She turned her face up to his, still asleep in his arms. The stress lines around her mouth and eyes had faded through the night. Blond hair caught along her bottom lip, and Kendric brushed it back to get a better view. Absolutely beautiful. Intense, secretive even, but beautiful. She was right before. About Penny. The four-year-old had Campbell's eyes and blond hair, but the rest came from him, and the possibility of having both beauties in his life thawed his icy rejection of the idea he'd able to have a normal life. A family. That he deserved to be happy.

He could be happy with them.

The thought took him by surprise. The past four days had turned his entire life on its head. He'd run from Loveland, from the ATF in Denver, from the people who'd cared about him, from a daughter he hadn't known existed, and he'd ended up nearly right back where he'd started. With Campbell. Faced with the same choice all those years ago after the bombing, Kendric knew what he wanted to do this time.

Blue eyes blinked up at him, followed by a wide, close-lipped smile. Her fingers grazed the skin above his T-shirt collar, light and electric. "How long have you been staring at me without my knowing?"

"Not long." And he still couldn't look away.

"I get the feeling that's a generous estimate of time." Staring down the length of their bodies intertwined, Campbell stretched as much as the small twin bed would allow before looking back up at him. "How's the arm?"

His initial response would've compared this wound to the ones he'd sustained after the bombing, but for the first time—ever—he held back. A single event had changed the course of his entire life, but was there any point in living the rest of it in fear and bitterness when there was so much more he hadn't experienced? Warm skin slid against him as he considered all his resentment had granted him. Isolation. A hefty weight of anger. Hollowness. Loneliness. How long before it consumed him completely? Where did that path end? "Sore, but better."

"Good." She peeled herself from his side, and he immediately missed her extra warmth. She'd always run colder than him. It was why they'd never been able to share blankets in the same bed. He'd preferred to sleep with a sheet while she'd taken possession of every comforter she could buy on a good Black Friday sale. She'd lost her jeans in the middle of the night, leaving her legs bare and flawless aside from the wool socks climbing her shins. The T-shirt she'd borrowed from Dr. Pascale brushed the tops of her thighs, giving him the perfect view of lean muscle as she bent to collect her jeans. She straightened and closed her eyes.

"You okay?" Kendric moved to sit up, but his shoulder took the fight right out of him. He collapsed back. Hell. How was he supposed to bring Sabrina Bryon in when he couldn't even get himself out of bed?

Campbell finished dressing. "I can already smell bacon. I swear Karie Ford is going to single-handedly be responsible for me failing my next physical fitness test."

"Yeah. She's good at that." He rubbed at the bruises darkening across his chest. "I once tried to tell her I would only have a grapefruit for breakfast after a late night. From the look she gave me, I thought she might not let me come back."

"Is it always like this?" She stared out the small cabin window over the kitchen sink, morning light brightening the shadows under her eyes. "The big family meals, letting perfect strangers borrow clothes and jackets and boots. The teasing and jokes and laughter. It's November, and there's already a Christmas tree set up in the main house like we're in some holiday mystery movie. I mean, come on. This can't be real. It can't last with the way things are going for this town. You have to know that."

Kendric considered her question. Not the words, but her tone, the way she talked with her broken and scraped-up hands. A surge of energy helped him from the bed, and he rounded to stand in front of her. A desperation took hold in her eyes as though she needed him to tell her the truth about this place, but there wasn't anything he could say that she didn't already know for herself. "It bothers you, what we have here."

"Yes." Campbell shook her head. "No. I don't know. It's just not like any department I've come across. You guys act like you're part of this family, and I'm…" She laughed. "I don't know what I'm saying, and it doesn't really matter. I'll bring you back something to eat."

She maneuvered around him, but Kendric caught her arm, turning her into his chest. Right where he needed her. Close. Part of him. He threaded his uninjured hand through her hair as her fear solidified in her expression. "You feel it, too."

"Feel what?" she asked.

"That Battle Mountain is special." He didn't know how else to explain it. "This place… It's not just somewhere I accidentally came across as part of my investigation into Agent Freehan. It's become part of me as much as it's part of the Fords and the Ingars and anyone else who grew up in this town." The truth resonated deeper than he thought it would. "For the first time since I left Loveland, I feel at home. Like I belong, and I'm not ready to give that up. You and Penny… Your lives are in Denver. I don't want to take that away from you. Your parents and the rest of your support system are there, but…"

He wasn't sure he had the courage to reveal the need clawing at him from the inside.

"But, what?" Campbell tugged free of his hand, standing up to him in her own right. So close. Reachable. Yet still guarded.

"But after everything that happened with Sabrina Bryon, after she took you…" He could still feel the tension down his spine, echoes of the panic, of the desperation to get to Campbell. He never wanted to feel that way again. Losing her once had been hard enough. Part of him had always had hope for reconciliation, but if her abductor had followed through, that would've been the end of it. He wouldn't have had anything left but a daughter who didn't know his face, and a lifetime of regret and guilt. "I realized I wasn't ready to let go of you again. Either of you."

"What are you saying?" Her eyes glittered with hope. Campbell stepped into him, notching her chin higher.

"I'm saying my time here in Battle Mountain might be coming to an end." His gut clenched. While he'd set out to find a new normal after the bombing had stolen half the feeling in his face and then to make up for the sins of the ATF, Kendric couldn't give up the opportunity to be part of Penny's life. Or start each day waking up next to the striking missing persons investigator he'd never forgotten. He couldn't give up the chance for happiness. "Once this investigation is concluded, I want to come home. For good."

A wide smile brightened her face, and Campbell crushed her mouth to his, careful of his arm in a sling. She intertwined her fingers with his and pulled him toward the door. "Then we better see about wrapping up this investigation."

After donning their boots and coats, they stepped out into the blistering cold and crossed to the main house hand in hand. As natural a feeling as he'd ever known, her connected to him like this. It had snowed more than a few inches overnight, and the flakes were still coming down. Campbell kept a watch out for compacted ice for both of them, catching him once as they neared the steps leading up to the front porch. The door hissed open before Campbell had a chance to knock, and a wall of warmth invited them inside.

Karie Ford ushered them in with hurried motions as they kicked snow from their boots to keep from tracking sludge inside. A knowing light glimmered in the Ford matron's eyes. "It's about time you two finally got out of bed. Come on now. Everyone's waiting."

Kendric rounded into the main room, complete with bearskin rugs, mounted animal heads and hand-carved bear statues. Old tile that had seen better days spread through the two-story living room, dining room and kitchen, but it wasn't the age of the house that had him considering turning around. It was the six sets of worried eyes on him and Campbell that clenched his insides. "What?"

"Here, dear." Karie Ford handed him a fresh mug of coffee. "You look like you need this more than I do."

He took the coffee, letting the heat chase back the dread solidified at the base of his spine.

Chief Ford's gaze slipped to Campbell and back, her shoulders slightly straighter than a moment before. The youngest Ford brother anchored his arm over Dr. Chloe Pascale and their newborn son in her arms at the far end of the massive oak dining table. "You good?"

"Never better." Kendric took a seat he'd claimed as his the past few times he'd been inside the main cabin, the weight of his department's study pressurizing between his shoulder blades. He leaned back in his chair as Karie Ford set a steaming plate of biscuits and gravy in front of him and poured him a fresh glass of orange juice. She definitely knew a way to a man's heart. "You going to stare at me all during breakfast, or are you going to tell me what's on your mind?"

Campbell slid into the seat beside his, her own mug in hand. "Something happened."

"We just got word." Alma Majors folded her arms across her chest, leaning into her partner on her right side. She glanced at Cree before turning her attention back to Kendric and Campbell. "Elliot Bryon just checked himself out of St. Mary's Medical Center."

"HOW IS THAT POSSIBLE? He was shot point-blank twice in the chest four days ago." Kendric rolled his shoulder forward, and instant pain contorted his expression. "I can barely stay on my own two feet from a single bullet wound in my shoulder."

Campbell slid her fingers down his uninjured arm, interlocking her fingers along the backs of his.

"We're not sure." Chief Ford looked to each one of them, and in that instant she saw a man who'd shouldered the well-being of this town for years on his own. A man who liked to test the truth for himself, who would do anything to defend Battle Mountain and the people he cared about against threats. Including an internal investigation into his department. In that way, they were alike. They each

believed in procedure, protocols and the law.
The way Weston Ford glanced out the window every minute or so said he always kept
himself on alert and reminded Campbell of
herself. They were realistic, always asking
questions and trying to learn as much as they
could about any given subject that would help
their agenda. But living like that was exhaust-
ing. She would know. "The two officers Grand
Junction PD posted on his room didn't even
see him leave. They're checking with hospital security and going over surveillance as we
speak. My guess, Elliot Bryon waited until a
shift change and took advantage of the distraction."

Her instincts flared. She'd always been good
at reading people. It was what made her one of
CBI's top Internal Affairs investigators, and,
considering she and Chief Ford followed a similar line of thinking, she had no doubt where
this conversation would lead. Campbell fit her
hands around her mug. "You think Sabrina
Bryon had something to do with it."

"You tell us. You're the only one here who's
had a face-to-face with her before the bullets
started flying." Easton Ford, in all his mus-
cular glory and sour attitude, locked his gaze
with hers as he raised a heaping spoonful of
oatmeal to his mouth. The former ranger had

a way of foreseeing problems before they occurred, a skill Campbell wished she'd acquired. But one that hadn't saved his fiancée's ability to walk after surviving a serial killer's attack. "Did she say anything to give you an idea she'd try to finish what she started with her husband and the woman he was sleeping with?"

"Not that I can remember. She had me drugged. Sodium thiopental. Like I said in my statement. There's not a whole lot I remember from our conversation." All eyes settled on her as though she commanded the floor, and a hint of nervousness pooled at the base of her spine. "But I can tell you, she's scared. She's on the run, a new mother without any support. She'll be sore and have very limited energy considering she had to deliver her daughter with no recovery time. She knows we're watching her phone activity and financials. She has no access to funds, and we haven't been able to determine any living family she can go to for help. Even with her training and background, she's out of her element."

"What background is that?" Cree Gregson narrowed his gaze on her. "Based on what we've put together so far, we can't even be sure if Sabrina Bryon is her real name."

"I'm not sure yet. I'm waiting for my sources

at CBI to get back to me, but I can tell you she's trained in our protocols. She's familiar with the law enforcement playbook, and she knows her way around this town. She can elude police for a long time," Campbell said. "What is the crime lab saying?"

"The blood you collected from the Bryon home belongs to Elliot Bryon, which isn't a surprise considering he took two bullets and nearly bled out in his own bedroom. Jane Doe has officially been identified as Rachel Stephenson, a parts manager for the auto parts store Elliot Bryon owns. Chloe was able to compare dentals from Dr. Corsey a few hours ago." Chief Ford nodded to his new wife and mother of the son currently asleep in the coroner's arms. "For now, there's nothing in her background to suggest she was anything more than a casualty of an affair gone wrong, but we're still looking into other possibilities. The sample Isla Vach took of your blood, Detective, is identical to a batch of sodium thiopental that went missing from Sabrina Bryon's ob-gyn's office. As for Sabrina Bryon's baby, her ob-gyn verified Elliot Bryon is the father. Perfect DNA match."

"What doesn't match are the bullets recovered from Elliot Bryon during surgery to the one Isla Vach took from your shoulder, Kendric." Alma Majors set one elbow on the table and her chin in her palm. The Latina archeologist turned cop glanced at each of her fellow officers in turn. "Ballistics from Unified Forensic is still trying to ascertain if either weapon was used in any other crimes."

"Based off what Campbell has said about our suspect, Sabrina Bryon would've ditched the gun used to shoot her husband as soon as possible. She's too smart to let something like that lead us back to her, but without either gun, we have nothing solid to tie her to the death of Rachel Stephenson and Elliot Bryon's shooting." Kendric turned his attention on Campbell and squeezed her hand beneath the table, out of sight from the rest of his department. "One thing I know for sure, Elliot Bryon lied to us when we questioned him about the events in that house. He was too calm, almost calculated. He claimed he can't remember what happened. Either way, we need to find him."

Genevieve Alexander leaned forward. "You said Sabrina Bryon knows police protocols and has knowledge of forensics, but she's not a cop. We've already checked. Her fingerprints aren't registered in the database, but in Colorado, private investigators aren't required to register their prints. I can pull licenses when I get back to the office, if that will help."

A private investigator. It made sense. While most PIs tended to specialize in legal investigations and computer forensics, there were several who went the homicide investigation route. Had Sabrina Bryon been one of them? Possibly under a different name? There was only one way to find out, and it wasn't by pulling expired rosters of private investigators from Colorado's Department of Regulatory Agencies. "Thank you. That would be really helpful." Campbell released her hold on Kendric. "If you'll excuse me, I need to check in with my CO."

She didn't wait for an answer, heading for the front door, her phone in hand. Campbell raised it to her ear just before stepping outside in case anyone at the table decided to follow. "It's me," she said to herself. From the position of the dining room—staring out at the first three satellite cabins—she hadn't been able to get eyes on the sixth cabin. And neither had anyone else.

Her CO had no interest in Sabrina Bryon's whereabouts, in the death of a mistress or a witness on the run. In fact, she'd been instructed to sever contact until she had something concrete to bring home. And she would bring this home. Something was going on in Battle Mountain, and her entire career—Penny's future—depended on her proving it. Campbell ducked beneath the dining room window as she followed the perimeter of the main cabin, just as she had the night before. Only this time Chief Ford was more occupied with his department than her. Stuffing her phone in her coat pocket, she pulled a lock picking set she'd acquired when she'd first agreed to sign on with Internal Affairs.

Agreed was a strong word. *Forced* had a more truthful ring to it. Straightening, she climbed the small set of stairs leading up to the sixth cabin and inserted the torque wench low into the keyhole with the slightest pressure. Sliding the rake along the top of the hole, she pushed it as far into the lock as it would go. Blinding sunlight reflected off glistening snow as she searched for any signs of interruption. No one had followed her from the main house, but she still had to move quickly. Within a few seconds, she'd set all the pins in the lock and twisted the torque wrench as though she were simply unlocking the door with a key.

Hinges protested against her intrusion, but there was no hint of an alarm. Silent or otherwise. No sensors on the doors or windows.

Campbell closed the door behind her. This cabin had been meant to serve as a temporary location for Battle Mountain PD. Not Fort Knox. With the department's dispatcher able to work from home, there was no need for on-site personnel, either. A strain of guilt fired through her as she gazed back at the main cabin. She and Battle Mountain PD were on the same side. If corruption had taken hold of the small department and this town, she had to believe Kendric would want to know. She slipped her tools back into her coat pocket and faced the small living space covered by three equal-size workstations. The one with the most paperwork drew her closer. Chief Ford's. "Okay. Show me what you got."

Campbell took her seat in the slightly too tall office chair and tapped the keyboard. A log-in screen brightened on the monitor. "Password. Password. Password." Her mind panicked to supply the answer when a neon green sticky note came into focus. She ripped the note free from the bottom of the monitor and typed in the intricate and complicated password. She had to hold in a laugh. Thank goodness for sleep-deprived chiefs of police. "DontStealMy-Password."

She was in.

Hesitation gripped the back of her neck as

she located digital case files uploaded in the past year. It didn't take long to verify the information she'd already collected on three prior homicide cases here in Battle Mountain against the original reports filed by Chief Ford himself. Next, she skimmed through the department's finances, then background checks for each officer and BMPD's dispatcher, Macie Barclay. No payoffs. No bribes. In fact, it looked as though Chief Ford sacrificed his own salary to ensure his officers were paid first and foremost for their service. At least on the surface. "Come on. There's gotta be something."

Her fingers ached as she forced them across the keyboard. She pulled call history for the chief and his brother, Easton. Then Cree Gregson and Alma Majors. Nothing out of the ordinary. She reviewed personal finances for each officer in turn, the uneasy feeling in her gut taking hold.

It wasn't possible. No department she'd investigated had ever been this clean.

According to all available records, the men and women of this department had nothing to hide. No connection to any of the suspects arrested and sentenced over the course of the past year. No evidence of corruption or favors. No pension fund to embezzle from or speeding tickets to pursue. Nothing. After all this—her taking jurisdiction for the Sabrina Bryon case, facing the man who left her, surviving an abduction and breaking into BMPD's files—she had nothing.

Chapter Eleven

He couldn't make up for the past.

Kendric passed off the last dish from breakfast in the main house to Campbell, his fingers coming into contact with hers. Such a simple action but one that threatened to rip the world straight out from under him. Despite the bullet wound in his shoulder, he hadn't slept as well as he had the night before in years. Because of her. Her heat, her determination to protect the people she cared about, her drive to prove she could handle any task without an emotional break. She was reliable and beautiful and a challenging handful he wanted to take on. He always had.

"Missed a spot." She pointed out some crumbs on the bottom of the plate he'd handed her. "I know you think you can only clean the top of the plate because that's where the food goes, but that's not how Karie is going to see it when she pulls these out from the cabinet again."

"Hey, give me a break. I'm doing this one-handed." And he was paying the price for that much. The hole in his shoulder had started roaring the moment he'd been left without her touch at breakfast, but he couldn't hold her back from doing her job. "Anything new from CBI?"

"What?" She swiped the drying rag around the perimeter of the plate, her expression distant as though her mind was somewhere else entirely. "Oh, no. Not yet. One of my colleagues is looking back through name change records, but he hasn't found anything we can use. In my experience, most people who file to change their names don't vary from their originals. Makes it easier to remember. So I have him looking into *S* names changed in the past ten years. Could take a while."

Kendric finished cleaning the contentious plate a second time and passed it along to be dried, but something wasn't right. Not just the distance. He could count on that anytime Campbell found herself in the middle of an investigation. There'd been days when they'd been together when nothing he said got through. She'd lose herself completely in any given case. Staying up all night, reviewing files and notes all day. Especially the ones that involved crimes against children. For those, he'd just had to leave her to work, knowing any interruption would only increase her pressure to solve the case on her own. "You okay? If you're still hurting after the car accident, I can—"

"No. I'm okay. Thanks." She didn't look at him, consumed with her duty to clean and put away Karie Ford's serving dishes. One by one.

He turned off the water and tossed the dish brush into the sink. "I can see the wheels in your head spinning, Bell. I know when something is bothering you."

Campbell blinked up at him, a mere inch of space between them. He'd sure as hell gotten her attention. "What did you call me?"

He thought back, not exactly sure of his point. Then it hit.

"I called you... Bell." Kendric's weight nearly buckled, and he leveraged one arm against the counter to keep himself upright. He hadn't done that in a long time. His nickname for her had come to life on their second date all those years ago. She'd been skating in the middle of the ice rink, a physical glow emanating around her with her high-volt smile. It was then he'd known. He'd wanted to spend the rest of his life with her. They'd made love for the first time that night. In the frenzy of passion and mind-blowing sensation, he'd lost his mind and screamed the last half of her name. No one had ever called her Bell before. In that moment, he'd turned what they'd agreed would be a casual experiment into something special, and she hadn't allowed anyone else to use the nickname as long as they were together. Had that changed? "I'm sorry. It just slipped out."

"No, it's okay." She shook her head, fisting the drying towel on the counter. "I just had this flash of ice-skating and roasted almonds and going back to your place that night. It surprised me is all."

"You didn't answer my question." Kendric moved into her, forcing her to either stare at his feet or look up into his eyes. "What's bothering you?"

She chose to direct her attention over his shoulder, but the difference in height between them only meant she was choosing the ceiling over meeting his gaze head-on, and a sick feeling set up residence in his gut. "I'm not sure I want you to move back to Denver."

"That's...not what I was expecting." Kendric stepped back. If her words had carried physical weight, he would've landed on his ass and not been able to get back up. Confusion ripped through him as he reviewed every hour they'd been forced to work this case together.

No. Not forced. It had felt that way at the beginning, but now he couldn't imagine solving this case without her. Without her insight, her single-mindedness, her passion for saving lives, they wouldn't have gotten past the primary crime scene. "I don't understand. You're the one who urged me to reconsider staying here. You said you wanted me to come home, to have a relationship with Penny, that you still feel something for me. What changed? If I've done something wrong or offended you—"

"No. You didn't. You didn't do anything wrong. And I know I'm the one who proposed that you leave Battle Mountain and that you should come home and meet your daughter, and I still want that. I do." Campbell gripped his uninjured arm, then ran her thumb along his bicep. "It's just…"

"It's what, Campbell?" he asked.

Her gaze met his, and she lowered her voice as footsteps and movement increased in the cabin's main living space. "You're thriving here. I've met and talked with the people you work with, and I can hear how much they care about you in their voices. I see how much this town needs you. I didn't want to acknowledge it at first. I thought you coming here was your way of detaching from the world and hiding to punish yourself for all the things you couldn't fix, but it has nothing to do with the past at all. You're happy here. You made a life here. You genuinely believe you can make a difference to the people of this town, and I don't want to be the one to take that away from you."

He wasn't sure what he was supposed to say to that, what he was supposed to think. His instincts reminded him he'd once suspected an ulterior motive for her involvement on this case, but he'd ignored that drive in favor of bringing a missing young mother home. The stakes had changed since that first visit to the crime scene. They'd uncovered the truth. At least, what they understood of the truth, and now Campbell wanted him to stay in Battle Mountain in the name of his happiness. "And if I said I'd be happy in Denver with you and Penny?"

Her mouth parted, but Campbell didn't let any emotion escape her gaze. Because she was a professional. He had to remember that. "Then I wouldn't be able to stop you, would I?"

Hurried steps and shouts penetrated the small kitchen they'd sequestered themselves inside. Kendric rounded the corner to get a full view of the living room, Campbell at his side.

"What's going on?" she asked.

"I don't know." He headed for the front door just as Karie Ford maneuvered Genevieve's wheelchair down the hallway leading to the back of the house. Dr. Pascale carried her and Weston's son after them. No sight of the chief, Cree, Alma or Easton, but the box the Ford matron had dedicated to holding firearms just inside the front door had been emptied of everything but his and Campbell's weapons. "Come on."

Campbell retrieved her gun, released the magazine and slammed it back into place. Angling to get a better view through the windows on either side of the front door, she waited for him to arm himself. "Looks like your chief and the other members of your department are waiting for something. They've taken positions behind the satellite cabins."

She glanced back at him.

He motioned for her to get behind him as he wrenched open the front door. They stepped over the threshold one at a time. Crisp November air burned down his throat as he took in his fellow officers' positions. Campbell was right. Something had spooked them. He didn't wait for the surprise, heading straight for Chief Ford at the head of the pack.

"Chief, what's going on?" he asked.

"Spotted a pickup truck coming up the mountain. Same description as the one you detailed that ran you off the road two days ago. See for yourself." The chief handed off a pair of binoculars, then turned his back to the cabin, staying low. "Nail strips took out the tires just beyond the gate. Whoever it is, they're coming in on foot."

Kendric pinpointed the truck's location down the mountain. The driver's-side door had been left open, but the tree line prevented him from picking up any other signs of movement. Both front tires were flat against the combination of dirt and snow. Whispering Pines Ranch might've become Colorado's ultimate mountain getaway over the past year, but the Ford brothers had gone to great lengths to keep the uninvited off their property. He handed off the binoculars to Campbell to get a look for herself. "How long do we have?"

"Your guess is as good as mine," the chief said. "Could be minutes, could be hours. All depends on why they're here and what the hell they want."

"The truck belongs to Budd Ingar. Chelsea Ingar loaned it to Sabrina, and she used it to run us off the road, leading to Chelsea's arrest." Campbell lowered the binoculars between her crouched thighs. "Could be he wants reparations. For his truck and his wife."

"We're about to find out." Kendric caught movement in the tree line east of their posi-

tion and unholstered his weapon. The rest of
his department followed his example, taking
aim at the same spot.

And waited. Two seconds. Three.

"Don't shoot! I'm coming out unarmed!"
Sabrina Bryon stepped free from the cover of
trees, a soft bundle clutched to her chest. Dark
brown eyes took in the officers ready to take
her down. Then locked on Campbell. Obvious relief pushed tears into the woman's eyes.
"Detective Dwyer, I need your help."

"My real name is Samantha Horsley." Sabrina Bryon stared down at the baby girl nes-
tled against her chest with a love Campbell felt
down to her core. "I moved to Battle Mountain
from Las Vegas to find a man named Dean
Pratt."

"Why?" Kendric asked.

"I'm a private investigator. Although I guess
you could say my license has lapsed. I was
hired to find Dean by a woman he assaulted
and raped six years ago, but the closer I got, the
more dangerous it became for my client." The
woman on the trigger end of the bullet in Kendric's shoulder rocked back and forth in the re-
cliner in the Ford's living room as though she
belonged. "She started getting death threats in
the middle of the night. At one point she called

me to tell me she was being followed by a man she recognized worked for Dean. I had to back off or risk him tying up any loose ends."

"I know everyone in this town. There's no Dean Pratt around here," Weston Ford said.

"There wouldn't be. Not unless you saw a photo of Dean." Sabrina rolled her lips between her teeth. "It took me months and a lot of favors to find where he'd disappeared to, but I finally caught up to him five years ago."

"And you married him." Campbell's gut clenched. She raised her gaze to Kendric, knowing the danger Sabrina had put herself and her baby into by divulging this information. "Elliot Bryon is Dean Pratt."

"Yes." Another line of tears welled in Sabrina's eyes as she clutched her infant to her chest. "I didn't have anything to prove he'd assaulted my client. I had to get close to him. I had to do something. After a while it was easy to forget why I was here. He was charming. He had a drive to conquer me as strong as my drive to conquer him, and it turned into a game. He'd pursue, I'd resist. I'd pursue, he'd resist. Until we finally got what we both wanted."

"That sounds like it's more than just a job." Easton rubbed his fingers into thick eyebrows, upsetting the delicate pattern. "Chasing after a suspected rapist across state borders without a license to investigate in Colorado, getting close enough to the guy to not only sleep with him but marry him, have a child with him. How much farther were you willing to go to prove he hurt someone?"

Campbell inhaled sharply. She felt both sympathy and revulsion. This woman had married a criminal, one who'd victimized her own sister, knowing what he'd done.

"As far as I had to," Sabrina said.

Campbell softened her voice as she considered everything that had happened in the past few days. A private investigator wouldn't put her life—her child's life—on the line so easily. There had to be a deeper reason. "The client who hired you. She wasn't just any client, was it?"

"She was my sister." Sabrina traced her infant's cracked lips with the tips of her fingers.

"Was?" Kendric asked.

"Dead." That single name brought visions of bitterness, anger, resentment and grief all in one tone. Sabrina seemed to hold her baby tighter at the inherent evil crossing her mind. "She only lasted a week after he'd assaulted her. Internal bleeding in her uterus. The emergency room doctors never caught it and released her not knowing they were signing her death warrant. She dropped dead right in front of me, and I knew right then what I had to do."

Silence closed in around the new mother.

"So you came looking for him, hoping to catch him on something he could be charged with." Awareness of Kendric flittered down her spine, and Campbell wanted nothing more right then than to forget this investigation, to forget her assignment in Battle Mountain, to tell him the truth. That same bitterness Sabrina held for her sister's attacker had taken up too much of Kendric's life. And she was making it worse. Lies were dangerous. They spread like wildfires and could become just as irreversible. They'd already been through so much. She wanted him to be part of her and Penny's lives, but fear of the truth, of how he'd take her involvement with IA, had her second-guessing every decision she'd made since she'd stepped foot into that crime scene. What she wouldn't give to make it all go away, to give them a real chance. "Sabrina, tell us what happened with Elliot and Rachel Stephenson four days ago."

"Isn't it obvious? Dean—Elliot—found out the truth." Real fear widened Sabrina's eyes. "I don't know how. Maybe he found something connected to my past, or I said something he thought was off. It doesn't matter. All I know is I came home to find that woman and my husband waiting for me. They each had a gun. She was holding my pregnancy pillow, I assume to muffle any gunshots if she had to pull the trigger. He said he knew everything and that I couldn't prove anything if I was dead. I tried to reason with him. I tried to get him to consider his daughter's life. He didn't care. He just wanted to make me disappear."

"His mistress had the gun?" Kendric asked.

A humorless laugh escaped Sabrina's well-curated control. "Rachel Stephenson wasn't his mistress. She's just one of many who handle the jobs he doesn't want to do himself. As far as I was able to tell, she's on Elliot's payroll, but she doesn't report to him. Her bosses are using the auto shop to smuggle all kinds of things." Sabrina bounced the baby against her chest. "She was just there to make sure nothing went wrong."

"And when Elliot found out why you'd really come to Battle Mountain, you were a problem that needed to be dealt with." Kendric's voice dipped into dangerous territory.

"I wasn't going to let him kill me and our daughter. I went for Rachel's gun. There was a struggle, but I somehow got control of it. I ran out the back door." Sabrina closed her eyes. "I remember two shots. Elliot was shooting at me. I heard a groan, and I turned around to see

Rachel collapse, but I couldn't stop. He shot her. I circled around through the trees, staying out of sight, and got in the car. I drove out of there as fast as I could, and I didn't look back."

Campbell could see it all play out as though she were the terrified mother on the run.

"Where is the gun you took from the house now?" Chief Ford asked.

Sabrina drove her hand into the pile of ratted blankets against her chest and pulled the weapon free. Every officer in the room tensed in case she turned the gun on them, but Kendric stepped forward to collect it with an evidence bag. "I'm sorry about your shoulder. I just couldn't let you take her from me."

"How do we know any of this is true?" Cree Gregson asked. "You could've made it all up on the way here, for all we know."

"I wouldn't have come here if I didn't need your help. I know what I'm risking by turning myself in, but I didn't have any other choice. My baby... She's... Something's wrong." Sabrina turned dark eyes to Campbell. "Detective, you're a mother. You would do anything you had to, to protect Penny. Please, I don't know what to do. My milk supply is gone. I can't feed her, and she won't wake up to eat."

"It's the stress. For both of you." Campbell moved to take a seat beside the woman who'd abducted and interrogated her. She stretched out her arms. "May I?"

"Campbell." Kendric's warning tone hardened the muscles down her spine. "Can I talk to you in private?"

Her gut said it was a waste of time answering questions he wouldn't understand the answers to, but as partners, they had a responsibility to one another. A respect. She wouldn't break that. Not until she had to. "I'll be right back."

Kendric pulled her back into the kitchen, clear of his department and Sabrina Bryon. "What are you doing? That woman ran us off the road. She kidnapped and drugged you. Not to mention shot me. Now you want to help her?"

"Yes." She shrugged her shoulders in an attempt to soften the blow.

"Why?" he asked. "This woman married her sister's rapist. Doesn't that strike you as a little bit off? What makes you think she won't turn on you as soon as she gets the chance?"

"Because she's scared for her daughter's life, and I know exactly what that feels like." Those bleary-eyed, desperate memories of Penny's birth threatened to tear through her, but Campbell held strong. Her voice broke as she willed Kendric to feel what she'd felt. "I know the physical pain that comes with the thought of losing a piece of you. The fear. There isn't anything you wouldn't do to make it go away."

The anger he'd resurrected in her defense drained. Setting his uninjured hand on her hip, Kendric pulled her against his chest. "I'm sorry. I wasn't thinking."

Campbell held on to him as her legs threatened to give out. She was so tired. Of the distance between them, of keeping four years of their daughter's life to herself, of shouldering it alone. She stepped back but couldn't force herself to let go. "I know it doesn't make sense, and I don't expect you to understand, but I believe her. I believe she's telling the truth. In which case, you were right. Elliot Bryon—Dean Pratt—whoever the hell he is, lied to us. He tried to kill his pregnant wife and then called 911 before hiding Rachel Stephenson's body in that tree and shooting himself twice in the chest to make it look like Sabrina had snapped. It was a risky move that could have ended badly for him, but this man obviously has a huge ego and some skill."

His strong exhalation brushed against the underside of her chin. "As much as I don't want to admit it, the evidence supports her statement over his. So what do you want to do now?"

"The stress is draining Sabrina's milk supply. We need to take her into protective custody and have Isla Vach come back to the ranch to examine the baby." She studied their original suspect, felt the gut-wrenching anxiety emanating from Sabrina Bryon's every pore as BMPD waited for her to make one wrong move. "Based on what Sabrina said, I don't think Elliot Bryon will stop coming after her. He'll be checking hospitals and—"

Campbell's phone trilled, and she unpocketed the device from her coat. Unknown number. Swiping her finger across the screen, she brought the phone to her ear. "Dwyer."

"Detective, I'm glad you picked up," Elliot Bryon said.

She locked her gaze on Kendric and hit the speakerphone option on the screen. The hardness was back in his expression in an instant as he snapped for the other members in his department to get their attentions.

Chief Ford was instantly on the phone, most likely to his dispatcher, Macie, to run a trace, but considering how careful Elliot Bryon had been to this point, she knew it would be useless.

"Mr. Bryon, we just got word you checked yourself out of the hospital." Campbell infused a false sense of care into her words. "Is everything okay? Where are you?"

"You can drop the pretenses, Detective." Elliot's voice deadpanned. Nothing like that performance he'd given in the hospital. "I know Sabrina is with you. Or should I call her Samantha? It's hard to keep all the lies straight these days."

"What do you want?" Campbell asked.

"You have something I want," he said. "Funnily enough, I have something you want, too."

The line staticked a split second before a second voice pierced through the speaker. "Mommy?"

Cold shot through Campbell's veins. Gravity increased its hold on her body until she wasn't sure she would be able to keep standing. She clutched the counter to stay upright. "Penny?"

"Mommy, I want to go home," her daughter said.

"And you will get to go home." Elliot Bryon had taken control of the phone again. "Just as soon as your mommy gives me what I want. Bring me Sabrina and Penny gets to go home. You have two hours, Detective. Make them count."

The line went dead.

Chapter Twelve

He was already moving.

"Macie didn't have enough time to get the trace." Chief Ford's voice registered as some distant dream. Real but faded. "Detective Dwyer, with your permission, I'd like to—"

"Kendric?" Campbell called after him, but the waver in his name wasn't enough to slow him down.

Kendric closed the distance between him and Sabrina Bryon and her infant. "Where is he? Elliot. Where would he go?"

"I don't know." Sabrina shook her head.

"You're lying." The rage, the resentment, the bitterness—everything he'd tried to let go of these past few days—reared its ugly head. Fire back-drafted through his chest until all he saw was red. Desperation unlike anything he'd felt before exploded through him. "Where did he take my daughter!"

Silence infiltrated as the weight of his department's attention centered on him.

Sabrina's infant wailed, but nobody moved.

"Kendric." A warm hand slid over his forearm and turned him to face the blonde beauty he couldn't imagine disappearing from his life again. Campbell framed his face, forcing him to look her dead in the eyes. Those same hands that held him shook as though she were ready to break apart at any moment. "We are going to find her. We are going to bring her home, but we have to hold it together. For Penny. Do you understand me?"

"He took her." Three simple words had the power to destroy him.

"And we are going to get her back," she said. "Please, help me get her back."

"I've put together a list of properties Elliot owns over the past few years. It's not much, but it's a place to start. I'll send you the addresses." Sabrina got to her feet in his peripheral vision. "I'm sorry. I never meant this to happen. I just wanted justice for my sister, and I made a mess of it... I'm sorry."

"Chloe." Campbell released her hold but never detached her attention from him. "Sabrina's milk supply isn't enough for the baby right now. Could you please help them?"

"Of course. I have some formula in the diaper bag." The coroner ushered Sabrina toward the hallway and presumably into one of the back rooms, out of sight.

Kendric couldn't take his eyes off Campbell. Off her strength, her determination to keep them from shattering right here in the middle of the damn living room when their world was under attack, her ability to compartmentalize, even in the face of loss.

"The rest of you, could you please give us a minute?" she asked.

The other officers filed from the living room without questioning her motives or argument, and it was then Kendric saw the power she held over everyone she came into contact with. The power she held over him. They were left alone, but the disquiet in his blood had reached an all-time high.

"Tell me what to do." A fraction of the fear Campbell described during Penny's birth singed his nerve endings. He couldn't think straight. He could barely keep himself breathing. Every cell in his body urged him to charge out that front door and rip the world apart to look for his daughter. He wanted to do something—anything—to stop the echo of thoughts running through his head. What if he never got the chance to meet Penny? What if he was too late? What would her loss do to Campbell? To him? What would losing their daughter do to them? "Tell me how to get her back."

"You can't." Campbell slipped her hand into her coat and pulled her phone free. She scrolled to a contact he couldn't read and tapped the screen. "But I know someone who can."

Confusion threatened to tip him over the edge. "What do you mean?"

"This is Officer Campbell Dwyer." She listed off her badge number. "I need a unit sent to my parents' address on file to make sure they're okay. My daughter has been kidnapped and is being held by a suspect considered armed and dangerous. Send an EMT." She gave them Elliot Bryon's details. "Have units search my home as well. Victim is four years old. Her name is Penny Dwyer. I'm sending a photo to you now."

"Officer?" Kendric didn't understand. She was a detective in the missing persons bureau of CBI. Not an officer. "Campbell, what's going on?"

"Yes, please transfer me." Campbell didn't move, didn't even seem to breathe. "Sir, I need a trace on a call that just came to my cell phone. Six minutes ago. Source is a man named Dean Pratt, operating under the alias of Elliot Bryon. He's holding my daughter hostage in exchange for his wife and infant." She shook her head. "Sir, we don't have time—"

A muffled voice intensified on the other side of the line.

"No, I understand you wanted no contact, but I—" Campbell raised her gaze to his, the color washing from her face. "No, sir. I have not uncovered any evidence of corruption or misconduct in Battle Mountain. As far as I can tell, BMPD has no influence over the violent events that have occurred here in the past year."

Misconduct. Corruption. Connection. The words tornadoed through his head until they became a single syllable he couldn't pick apart. Heat flared through his gut, and Kendric stepped back.

"Thank you, sir. I'll be waiting for your call." Campbell disconnected, her phone still in hand. "Kendric—"

"You're Internal Affairs." The words clawed free from the box he hadn't been willing to look inside since she came back into his life. A part of him had known. Not the specifics, but that there was something else at play here. Something he couldn't let go of. Now he knew. His instincts had been right. "All this time, you made me think you were here to recover Sabrina Bryon, that you were a missing persons agent here to help, but you had your own agenda. You were sent here to spy on my department. On me."

"Yes." Such a simple answer but one that held influence to obliterate entire lives. "CBI sent me to assess BMPD. I didn't choose it, Kendric. I was told to join IAB or lose my career. I did what I had to, to provide for our daughter. I never intended any of this to happen, but that's not what's important right now. Penny is out there with a psychopath who will hurt her if we don't do something to stop him."

"Don't give me that." He couldn't contain the spiral pulling him beneath the surface. A low ringing pierced his ears as the future they'd built together these past few days faded. "You and I both know there's not a damn thing in this world that can force you to do something against your will. You had a choice. You chose wrong."

Campbell let her mouth part. "Do you think I don't worry about that every day I'm on the job? That I don't lie awake at night wondering if the men and women I investigate will try to get revenge on me or Penny or my parents? I didn't want this, Kendric, but I did what I had to, to survive being a single parent."

"Is Penny even mine?" He hadn't meant to ask, but it was too late to take it back. "Or was that a lie, too? A play to pull me in, to get me to fall for your lies and trust you?"

Her voice barely reached across the few feet between them. "You really think so little of me I'd lie about our daughter?"

"I don't know what to think of you, Campbell," he said. "I don't know you. Maybe I never have." Kendric headed for the front door. His phone chirped with an incoming message. The list of Elliot Bryon's properties Sabrina had offered to supply. Whether Penny was his or not, a four-year-old girl was out there. Alone. Scared. She wanted nothing more than to go home to her family, and Kendric had the duty to make that happen. He'd search every address on the list if he had to. No matter how long it took. He collected his weapon from the storage by the front door and holstered it at his side.

"Where are you going?" she asked.

He thought the answer was obvious. "To find your daughter."

"You don't even know where Elliot Bryon is keeping her. You could be wasting time, and that's not something I'm willing to risk. My CO will call back with a location after the computer squad finishes the trace. Look at me." Campbell squeezed her hand around his arm. "It's not solely up to you to bring her home. We have to work together. Penny needs us."

"Us? There is no us." His skin burned with her touch, and Kendric pried his arm from her grip. "The day I partner with the rat squad is the day I stop being a cop. You're not police. You're a glorified hall monitor hell-bent on ending careers. You want to know why I came to Battle Mountain, why I signed up to help this town? Because of the men and woman in that other room. They protect each other. They're honest with one another. They're a family, and they would never turn on each other for a paycheck. Ever. And you… You're nothing like them. Penny deserves better, and so do I."

He regretted the words the moment they'd left his mouth.

Campbell stepped back, that iron control slipping. Just for a moment, he recognized the woman he'd started falling for all over again. A momentary glimpse of her heart and all the reasons he'd wanted her to be part of his life. "You don't get it, do you? Why I'm here instead of another IAB officer."

"It doesn't matter." He stripped free of his arm sling and tossed it on the back of the worn leather couch stretching in front of the fireplace where so many holidays, birthdays and family dinners had been spent. He'd bought his cabin after visiting Whispering Pines Ranch one time. That single visit had been enough for him to want his own place to create the warmth and safe haven this place provided, maybe even start a family to fill it with. He'd already envisioned Campbell and Penny on Christmas mornings, eating breakfasts at the table, cozying up on the couch in front of the fire at night. But that was all it was. A fantasy. "As soon as Penny is safe and the bastard who took her is behind bars, I want you gone. Forever."

"Don't do this again, Kendric." Tears welled in Campbell's eyes, but they wouldn't have a hold on him this time. "You don't understand."

"No, that's the problem, Campbell. I understand everything. You lied to me. You got close to me, and you used me to investigate my department, and I fell for it. I should've seen the truth. I should've known you were more interested in closing your case than being with me. Because who would want to be with someone like this?" His scars burned as though aware of his accusations. "You made a choice when you came here, and it sure as hell wasn't us."

"You're right." Her face voided of expression. She'd already detached from him. As though she'd simply switched off a light. So easy. It was like Elliot Bryon had said. What was the point of keeping up pretenses when the truth had come into the open? "Why would I want to be with someone as angry and bitter and distrusting as you?"

He stepped out into the freezing day. Elliot Bryon had taken his daughter. And Kendric was going to get her back. With or without Campbell's help.

He was gone.

Again.

Campbell stared after a pair of blurry brake lights out the cabin's front door as Kendric made his way down the mountain. All the things he'd said, the accusations—her heart gripped in her chest and refused to let up. *Penny deserves better, and so do I.*

Footsteps reverberated up through her from the old hardwood floors. Chief Ford and his Battle Mountain officers had heard every word between her and Kendric. She closed her eyes, willing this moment to stretch as far as possible to avoid what came next. But reality didn't always work the way she wanted.

"The night I ran into you outside. You weren't enjoying the fresh air, were you?" Chief Ford's voice warned her answer would decide her fate in this small town she'd come to love. "You were running your own investigation."

"It sounds like you already have your answer, Chief." Campbell pried herself away from the window, slid her hands into her coat pocket and unpocketed her credentials. She tossed them his way.

He caught them against a broad chest, never once taking his gaze off her. None of them did. Easton Ford and his fiancée, Genevieve. Cree Gregson and Alma Majors. Even Dr. Pascale. This…family that had supported Kendric the past few months, who'd fed her, clothed her, talked to her like a human rather than a rat. They deserved answers. Answers she couldn't give. "Officer Campbell Dwyer. Internal Affairs Bureau of CBI." He threw her badge and credentials back. "So, Officer. Did you get what you came for?"

Such a simple question. But one she didn't have an answer for. She'd come to this sleepy mining town for an assignment, but she'd uncovered so much more along the way. A department of men and women who treated each other more like siblings than colleagues. A town that felt more like home than Denver ever had. A man she'd imagined spending the rest of her life with, who accepted her and protected her. A sense of purpose she hadn't ever experienced in her position with CBI or any other job. All of it had been within reach, just for a moment. And it was slipping through her fingers. "I won't be pursuing my internal investigation into BMPD, if that's what you mean."

"Then the Sabrina Bryon case is no longer under CBI jurisdiction." Easton Ford stepped to the front like a true alpha male protecting his pack. "It looks like you're done here, Detective."

But she wasn't. Not yet. And running with her tail tucked between her legs had never been part of her personality. "Listen, I understand none of you may respect what I do. You may not even like me, but you don't know my reasons for doing what I did, and you don't know me. My daughter is everything to me. She is the only thing that motivates me to do my work, and she's out there right now being held by a man from your town. Whether you like it or not, that makes him both of our problems, and I'm not leaving Battle Mountain without her. So you can either help me find Penny, or you can stay out of my way."

"We're Battle Mountain police, Officer Dwyer. We swore to protect this town and everyone in it, including you. We'll do whatever it takes to bring your daughter home." Chief

Ford maneuvered past her toward the front door, his officers filing behind him. "As for what went down between you and Kendric, you're on your own." He turned to his wife. "Alma will stay with you and Sabrina Bryon until Isla can check her and the baby out. I'll be on the radio in case you lose cell service and need to get a hold of me." He kissed her, then his son before slipping out the door.

Easton Ford crouched beside Genevieve's wheelchair, saying nothing. It was as though they could read each other's minds when he pressed his forehead to hers. The district attorney held on to his hand as long as possible before she was forced to let go, and Campbell's heart pinched.

Even Gregson seemed to have a hard time letting go of his partner.

That kind of love only came around once in a lifetime. And she'd ruined her chances of earning it for herself. Campbell reached for her weapon from the storage bin just inside the main house's front door as BMPD dispersed to their vehicles. Stepping out into the frigid night, she braced herself against the cold working through her. Not from the dropping temperatures or the flakes falling from the sky. From the emptiness she couldn't seem to shake.

At missing Penny. Fearing for her.

At knowing Kendric would never look at her the same again.

At losing the future she'd started to imagine. Just the three of them.

She cut through deepening snow as Kendric's department pulled their vehicles down the long driveway to head back to town. Kendric had brought her to Whispering Pines Ranch. Her rental had probably started collecting parking tickets on Battle Mountain's Main Street where she'd left it four days ago, and getting lost down the mountain as a storm closed in wasn't going to help Penny in the least. She needed a vehicle.

The growl of an engine cut through the silence pressurizing the air in her lungs. Headlights illuminated glistening snow as a pickup seemingly built for war curved into the driveway. Campbell shielded her eyes as the spotlights centered on her. The driver's-side door opened. "You know there's a truck with two flat tires down the road? I nearly ran into a tree trying to avoid it on the way up here."

Isla Vach, the EMT Chief Ford had called to tend to Kendric's wound, hopped down from the oversize monster that didn't fit her personality at all. Followed by a smaller version of the brunette a moment later. "You've got another patient for me, Detective Dwyer? Wait. Did Kendric tear his stitches? I warned—"

"No. He's fine, and thanks again for helping him. The chief wanted you to take a look at someone else. Sabrina Bryon and her baby are inside. Officer Majors can give you all the details." Campbell studied the resemblance between the EMT and the girl who'd climbed down from the passenger seat. "Is this your daughter?"

"Yeah. Mazi, this is Detective Dwyer. She's helping the police with an investigation." Isla pulled her girl closer, back to front, with obvious pride in her smile.

"Wow! Do you solve crimes like my daddy?" Mazi asked.

"Um, yeah. I do, but not the kind you're thinking of." Campbell's own smile stretched across her mouth as she compared Penny's four-year-old attitude against the girl in front of her. Her daughter hadn't bothered to ask what Campbell did to keep a roof over their heads. Penny's entire world was currently dictated by her next snack. It was the most frustrating thing to keep having to go to and from the pantry dozens of times throughout the day, on top of cooking meals, but Campbell wouldn't give it up for the world. Tears burned as her determination to hold it together cracked. She had to be strong. For Penny. It was the only way to get her back. "What does your daddy do?"

Instant regret stabbed Campbell in the gut as smiles fell from Mazi's and Isla's faces. "I'm sorry. I didn't mean to pry."

"No. It's okay. We lost my husband on his last tour to Morocco a few months ago." The EMT scrubbed her hands up and down Mazi's arms. "A government-sanctioned weapons deal that went bad. I don't really know all the details."

A tear escaped Campbell's control, and her heart threatened to beat straight out of her chest. "I'm sorry for your loss."

"Us, too. Anyway, it looks like the entire department was headed someplace. We won't hold you up. Have a good night, Detective." Isla maneuvered her daughter toward the main cabin.

"Isla, wait." Campbell turned after them. "Is there any way I could borrow your truck for a few hours? I wouldn't normally ask a complete stranger, but it's an emergency." Her gaze dropped to Mazi. "I have a daughter, too, and right now, she needs me more than ever."

Isla tossed the keys. "We're not strangers. Us moms have to stick together."

"I'll take good care of it. Thank you." She didn't wait for a response, pumping her legs as hard as two feet of snow would allow. Climbing into the massive truck, Campbell got behind the wheel and headed down the mountain. She didn't know where she was going. Didn't know if her CO would ever get back to her with Elliot Bryon's location, but she couldn't sit around and wait. She had to do something.

Her phone chimed from her coat pocket. An incoming message.

She hit the brakes and pulled off the side of the slushed-out road leading to the highway that would take her back in to Battle Mountain. The screen illuminated the inside of the cabin. Her CO had come through. The bastard who'd taken her daughter had called from a property on the outskirts of town. Not too far. She went to send the information to BMPD but didn't have any of their contact information. Dialing 911, Campbell relayed the location to Macie Barclay and prayed the dispatcher would get it to them in time. She hung up. "Got you."

Campbell tossed her phone into the passenger seat and pushed back onto the road. If she lost Penny... No. She was going to make it. There was no other option. "Keep it together, Dwyer. Just a little while longer."

The miles passed in a blur, but the closer she came to her destination, the tighter she held the steering wheel. Elliot Bryon had assaulted, raped and ultimately killed one woman before trying to murder another. She couldn't risk a direct approach and force the psychopath to cut his losses. She needed another plan.

Campbell brought the truck to a stop a quarter mile from her final destination and switched off the headlights. Night had already consumed any outline she might've been able to see at this distance during the day, but her gut said there was something worth investigating up ahead. There was no sign of Battle Mountain PD. She couldn't wait. "I'm coming, baby."

She hit the icy pavement and closed the driver's-side door as softly as possible. Elliot Bryon was smart. He'd evaded authorities this long. He wasn't going to take any chances of letting someone just walk onto his property, and neither was she. The terrain flattened once it dipped off the road and spread out into never-ending fields on either side. Not a whole lot of places to take cover, but she didn't have any other option.

Staying low, Campbell jogged a few yards off the main road. Snow and ice worked into her boots. Numbness had already started in her fingers, but she kept her index finger over the trigger of her sidearm. Within a few minutes, she'd gotten close enough to the property to make out the dark shape of a structure ahead. A long outline with a pitched roof. Striations cleared as her vision adjusted to the dark. Not a residence or a warehouse. But old. Something original to the area. She cut across the landscape to a small growth of trees ahead and took cover.

Lights glimmered from vertical windows across the front. Patches of dark soil or volcanic rock peeked through the snow leading to the front door. Recently used. Penny was here. She could feel it. Tightening her grip around her weapon, Campbell took a step closer.

Her boot caught on something, and she tipped forward. She slammed into a tumbleweed, cutting her palm on the same kind of volcanic rock leading up to the structure. Pain ignited through her broken hand. What the hell?

Swallowing a groan, she tugged the line free of her bootlaces. Fishing line. Why… Warning exploded in her gut, and Campbell shoved her heels into the ground to propel her forward.

She slapped her hand over her weapon.

A split second before a man's boot pressed down to stop her. "Hello, Detective. Penny's been waiting for you."

Chapter Thirteen

He'd already gone through four addresses from Sabrina Bryon's list of her husband's holdings. Every single one of them empty.

There were at least twenty locations left. He couldn't do this all night. Not when Penny's life was at stake. Damn it. He should've waited for a location from Campbell's CO. He'd just been so angry, betrayed. Now he was out in the middle of nowhere hoping to stumble upon his daughter and bring her home.

"Hell." Kendric put the SUV in Park and stared out across white-covered farmland through the windshield. Campbell's parting words had drilled into his brain and wouldn't let up. *Why would I want to be with someone as angry and bitter and distrusting as you?* That had been it, hadn't it? All this time, since the moment she'd interfered in his case, he'd wanted to prove he was more than the defective former ordinance tech, the failed ATF instructor, the has-been. That he could be someone she would respect and love. Someone she'd be proud of, someone worthy of her fire and commitment. He scrubbed a hand down his face to clear the bleariness and exhaustion from his eyes. "You screwed that up."

No. She was the one who'd lied. She'd kept him in the dark about her real agenda for coming to Battle Mountain, made him feel balanced, good. Like she cared about him. It had all been a lie. He knew that now, but knowing one thing and accepting it were two completely different things. Still, a part of him had longed for it to be true. There'd been countless minutes he'd watched her while she'd slept next to him in that too small cabin at the ranch, imagining the three of them together. Him, Campbell and Penny. They'd get their own place. Not his here in Battle Mountain or hers in Denver. Someplace new that they could grow into and make their very own. A fresh start.

Wasn't going to happen now, though.

Their lives were headed in two different directions. His as a reserve officer and hers doing everything in her power to sabotage the very departments she was supposed to support. He didn't really believe that. He'd said it—to her and to himself—at least a dozen times, but the truth was, he knew why she'd joined

Internal Affairs. And it hadn't been to put a roof over their daughter's head. He just hadn't wanted to admit it to her or anyone else. But the investigation into what happened the day the bomb had taken almost half of his face and injured a dozen other techs hadn't given her any excuse to lie to him.

He shifted the SUV into Drive and maneuvered back onto the main road. Something heavy slid under the passenger seat. Glass shattered, and Kendric braked on the isolated road. "What the hell?"

He shifted across the center console and felt around for whatever it was, the floor sopping wet. The hole in his shoulder screamed as it pressed against the steering wheel. Then his hand. He pulled back, watching a line of blood trail down the side of his middle finger. Angling over the passenger-side seat, he grabbed for the glove box and pulled a fresh tissue from inside. Along with his flashlight. Dark upholstery peppered with glass brightened under the beam, and Kendric realized what had broken beneath the seat. Slowly slipping his hand between the adjustment bars, he tugged the base of Campbell's snow globe free. The one Sabrina Bryon had taken from her luggage at the motel and mounted to the hood of her rental with a note.

Fake snowflakes clung to the sides and stuck to his fingertips. The glass had been destroyed thanks to his driving skills, but the insides looked all right. He checked out the gingerbread house decorated with icing and gumdrops, and the small gingerbread couple too large to fit inside their house. Peppermint candies lined the rooftop and the pathway leading to the front door, and Kendric had the slap of déjà vu. Of him picking it out just for her in the overpriced boutique Campbell had talked about visiting during Christmas one year. He'd gone without her, hoping to surprise her. And he'd succeeded that first holiday they'd been together. She'd loved it.

Hell. She'd kept it. No. She hadn't just kept it but had brought it with her on an assignment to Battle Mountain. And he'd been an idiot. "Son of a bitch."

She'd been telling the truth. Not about her assignment from Internal Affairs but everything else. She'd had no intention of using him to investigate his fellow officers. She'd wanted him to come home.

He set the remnants of the globe on the passenger seat and pulled his phone. Dialing Chief Ford, he stared at the perfect gingerbread world around shards of glass lined with his blood. The line rang once. Twice. He didn't wait for the chief's greeting as the call connected. "I need to talk to Campbell."

"Then you've got the wrong number, buddy," Chief Ford said.

"I don't have her number." Which was probably up there in the stupidest decisions he'd made over the past few days. "Just give her the phone...sir."

"That would be a great trick. After you left, Officer Dwyer asked us to help find her daughter. Last I heard, Isla Vach handed over the keys to her truck. Said Campbell had a daughter who needed her and took off. Cell service is getting weak with the incoming storm. Can't even get ahold of Macie."

Damn it. "How long ago?"

"Ten minutes, maybe less." Voices filtered from the other side of the line. Both feminine and male. "Listen, Hudson, I'll be honest. We weren't exactly thrilled she'd been sent to investigate the department. Words were exchanged, and I get the feeling Detective—Officer—Dwyer won't be back anytime soon. I've got Easton and Gregson out clearing roads, but I'm still doing a sweep of some of those properties Sabrina Bryon sent you. If we come across her, I'll let you know."

The snow was coming down harder now, and a chill went through him. Denver saw snow, but it wasn't anything compared to this. Battle Mountain didn't have the personnel or the funds to maintain a fleet of snowplows. It was BMPD's responsibility to salt and clear the roads. One wrong move and Campbell could find herself hurt or worse. He had to find her. "You said Isla Vach lent Campbell her truck. Is there a GPS on that monstrosity?"

The pickup had belonged to her late husband, a military man, who'd put everything he had toward keeping his family safe and supplied. A prepper in every sense of the word. That truck had doubled as a bunker, from what Kendric had heard. Fully stocked with supplies, ammunition, a weapon, blankets and extra fuel. A lot of money had gone into it. The man would've made sure he knew where it was at all times, even while on deployment.

"Isla's at the ranch with Majors, Chloe and Sabrina Bryon and the baby. Hold on. I'll check." The line cut out. Seconds ticked by across the screen, every moment more tense than the last. The chief came back on the line. "You were right. The truck is equipped with GPS. I'll send you the coordinates and redirect there. Until then, I want you to be careful."

"Thanks, Chief." He disconnected, more on edge than the second preceding an explosive tearing across his face. Campbell had gone after Penny. Without backup. The snow globe rocked gently in the passenger seat as he accelerated back onto the road. The storm had arrived. It was only a matter of time before it would white out everything in sight.

His phone pinged. A message from the chief. With an address containing the last known location of Isla Vach's truck. Recognition flared as he recalled the list Sabrina Bryon had sent him. It was the same address as one of the listings toward the bottom, one he might not have gotten to in time without the chief's help. Campbell had to be there. Kendric floored the accelerator, risking going off the road, but time was already running out. If she'd found Penny, there was no telling what Elliot Bryon would do when he realized she hadn't held up her end of the deal in handing over Sabrina and his daughter. The man was dominating, angry and relied on a survival instinct more volatile than any offender Kendric had come across. Campbell didn't have a chance.

He wasn't going to lose her again.

He loved her, damn it.

Despite the fact that Campbell had kept the truth from him, he loved her. He didn't want to see her or Penny hurt. He'd gone five years without Campbell in his life, and there wasn't a single part of him that wanted to risk another five. Her job had nothing to do with her ability to care for their daughter, her determination to bring Sabrina Bryon home safely or to stop a madman from getting away with murder. Campbell stood as a testament to everything he wanted in his life and everything he'd been missing since he left her all those years ago. And he was going to bring her and Penny home. For good.

Falling snow stuck to his windshield and smeared with the aid of the wipers. According to another message from the chief, the GPS on Isla Vach's truck hadn't moved. He took the next turn too sharp, the back tires fishtailing out of alignment. The muscles in his jaw ached under the pressure of his back teeth. The coordinates landed outside of town, approximately a mile from the city center. Another area he hadn't taken the time to familiarize himself with the past few months. Didn't matter. He'd been trained in rescue and recovery. Only this time, there were two victims Kendric intended on walking away with tonight.

The engine of his SUV coughed as the readout on the dashboard dropped below ten degrees. All Battle Mountain PD vehicles were equipped with emergency supplies. Fuel, blankets, Kevlar vests, shovels and calorie bricks. Nothing that would keep the engine warm.

The vehicle jerked forward without instruction. "Come on. Don't do this. Not now."

Too late. The engine sputtered twice more, then died. He tried to wrestle the wheel as the power steering gave out, and tapped the brakes. Within a few hundred feet, he was stalled. Headlights expanded out in front of him. Nothing but deep snow and dead trees in the distance. Every second he wasted was another second Campbell and Penny didn't have. Grabbing for his phone, he tried to pick up a signal. "A dead spot. Great. You wanted to be on your own all this time, you got it."

He didn't have any other choice. He couldn't leave Campbell to deal with Elliot Bryon alone. Not when their daughter's life hung in the balance. Kendric shouldered out of the warmth of the SUV and stepped out into the cold. Zipping his jacket, he rounded toward the bumper and unhitched the cargo door. The fuel wouldn't do him a damn bit of good. Even anti-freeze had its limits in temperatures this low. The blankets would protect him from the thrashing winds, but it wouldn't be enough to keep his body temperature from dropping. That left the Kevlar vest. It was heavy. Not exactly something he wanted to pack around for the next two miles, but it was all he had.

Kendric strapped in, tightening the Velcro

over the wound in his shoulder. He locked up the vehicle and headed straight into the wind, a blanket wrapped around his middle and face. "Hang on, Bell. This isn't over."

JERKING MOVEMENTS BROUGHT her around.

The pain in her hand flared as Campbell forced her eyes open. Cold whipped at the exposed skin of her face and neck. She was still outdoors. A thick blanket of white eased down from the wide-open, velvety sky. Blistering winds dried her lips until the smallest movement pulled the split along the bottom apart. She tried to reach for a passing bush, but her fingers wouldn't obey her command. The boots Genevieve Alexander had lent her caught in a mixture of compacted snow and black rock. The building with the pitched roof, Elliot Bryon, the fishing line acting as a security system—it was all coming back now. "Penny."

"Don't worry, Detective. You'll see her soon enough." Elliot Bryon pulled her coat tight against her neck with each tug. He was dragging her.

Wood stairs cut into her spine as he hauled her into the structure, and Campbell hit the floor facedown. Warmth burned along her nerve endings against the cement floor, dust

kicking up with each exhalation off the surface. She notched her chin higher to get a view
of her attacker as he strode to the other side of
the open room containing two massive firepits.
Each had been lit and allowed to rage, and
an instant sweat built at the back of her neck.
"Where is my daughter?"

"Safe. For now." Elliot shouldered a rifle
while stoking the fire closest to her.

She could turn around right now. She could
run for the door. Get help. Storm this place
with backup and save Penny. But there was
no telling what Elliot Bryon would do to her
daughter in the meantime, if he'd even still be
here when she returned. She couldn't risk it.
No. This was it. It was now or never. For her
and her child.

"I wouldn't do that if I were you." A broad
smile pooled dread at the base of her spine.
Dark eyes glittered as bright as the embers
fleeing the flames a few feet from him. "I
might not look like much, especially with two
fresh wounds in my chest, but I can still hit a
moving target at three thousand yards."

Campbell rose to her feet, slower than she
wanted to get a lay of the building he'd brought
her to. No interior walls. Fire highlighting
every corner and the full wall of what looked

to be antique blacksmith tools. "What the hell do you want?"

"I told you what I wanted. You were to bring me Sabrina in exchange for your daughter's life. I thought I made that clear." He wagged his finger at her, no evidence of pain in his expression. "Although, I will give you credit for sticking to the two-hour time frame. In these situations, most people would have gone to the police and tried to bust in here, guns blazing. But you… You surprised me. You came alone." Elliot slid a strand of her hair behind her ear. Too close. Too intimate. "You must really love Penny."

She jerked away. "Touch me or Penny and those two holes in your chest won't be your only problem."

His laugh drilled through her confidence and filled every inch of the single room. "I like you. It's a shame you can't follow simple instructions, though. I didn't want to have to hurt Penny. She's sweet. Just like I envision my own daughter to be one day, but I did warn you what would happen if you failed to come through."

Elliot started walking away from her.

"You wouldn't." Campbell had to believe that. Despite the cases she'd investigated and the studies she'd reviewed, she had to believe that kind of evil couldn't touch her daughter. "She's just a child. This is my fault. This is my responsibility. She has nothing to do with this."

He turned to face her, one arm sweeping outward as though he'd taken center stage. "She has everything to do with this, Detective. Don't you see that? Without her, I don't have you, and without you, I don't have Sabrina. Without Sabrina, the people I answer to aren't going to be very happy." His expression hardened as he pulled the iron he'd used to stoke the fire free from its perch. Closing the distance between them, he positioned the hot metal in front of her face. "Now, you can either tell me where my wife is, or you can lose your little girl. The choice really is quite simple."

Heat licked along her neck and cheek. He wanted her to choose between her daughter and the woman and infant he'd tried to kill? She fisted her hands against the urge to lash out at him, to punish him for giving her such an impossible task. She'd joined the sheriff's department all those years ago to save lives. Even inside IA, she protected the public and police departments against corruption and misconduct. She couldn't just hand over Sabrina and her baby. Not when she'd experienced this man's anger firsthand. "I can't."

"Shame. In that case, I'm afraid we don't

have anything more to talk about." Elliot Bryon headed for a door she hadn't noticed until now, perfectly level and painted the same color as these old walls.

"No. You can't do this." Her head spun, from the violent change in temperature, the pain in her hand or losing Kendric all over again—she didn't care. He'd taken her gun, but she wasn't going to let him get away with this. Campbell ran for the wall organized with tools she'd never seen outside of television and movies set in medieval times.

A bullet whizzed past her arm and embedded in a small section of grating holding the tools in place a split second before she reached for one. "Now, come, Detective. You don't want this to get messier than it already has."

"I don't mind getting my hands dirty." Campbell ripped a hammer from the immaculately preserved collection. It was no match against the rifle in Elliot Bryon's hands, but her gut said she had to act fast enough to keep him away from Penny, wherever she was. "Do you?"

An amused smile flittered across his weathered and strong expression. He pressed his tongue against the inside of his bottom lip with a nod. "I knew there was something I liked about you." He didn't wait to give an official start and rushed her.

Campbell swung the hammer high, but her attacker caught her wrist. She knocked the rifle from his grip. It skidded across the floor, out of reach. A hard kick to her stomach shoved her back against the wall stocked with tools. They fell around her, bouncing off her shoulder, as air locked in her chest.

Elliot Bryon reached for the closest weapon, a metal poker stoking the fire to his right.

"Come on, Detective. You're better than this." Swinging the red-hot metal above her, he pried the hammer from her hand. He tossed it out of reach.

She couldn't lose. For Penny's sake. For hers. Campbell backed away from the burning rod and widened her stance. She'd trained in close quarters defense. She could do this. Forcing her lungs to work overtime, she lunged. She faked a head-on strike, then pivoted and rammed her fist into Elliot's gut. She heard the air crush from his lungs, but it didn't slow him down.

Pain ignited as the stoker connected with her arm. She jerked back. The momentum threw her off balance, and she hit the floor. A gut-wrenching kick to her ribs caught her off guard. Campbell rolled into the same wall to protect her organs. But it wasn't enough. She wasn't enough against him. She wasn't strong enough for Penny, for this town. For Kendric.

White pulses of light lined the edges of her vision. Tears burned in her eyes, but she wouldn't let them fall.

"You know, I'm actually quite disappointed, Detective. You hear about all these mothers desperate to save their children. So desperate they can lift cars or chase down the people responsible for hurting their kids." Heat flared and ebbed as Elliot Bryon prowled in front of her between her and the flames. Back and forth. Back and forth. "You… You're just like everyone else I've had to deal with. Weak. Penny deserves better, don't you think?"

Penny deserves better, and so do I. Kendric's words took her out of the moment. She'd come to Battle Mountain as an assignment and to find closure, but she didn't want closure. She wanted the man who'd tied himself to her through their daughter, who'd come for her when Sabrina Bryon had abducted and drugged her for information. The rational part of herself warned pursuing a future with Kendric would be a lost cause, but love wasn't rational.

Love.

She'd fallen back in love with him. Through

all the hurt, the loneliness, the secrets, he'd given her permission to just be…her. Intense, defensive, high-strung. She'd always been an outsider within her own department, with her friends, but none of that had stopped him from working his way back into her heart. He'd supported her despite his bitterness toward the world because maybe she'd left an impression on him, too. And that was worth living for.

Campbell fisted her uninjured hand. Proving her worth had nothing to do with her career as she'd convinced herself all these years. Yes, focusing on her job had been a way to put a roof over her daughter's head and to ensure Campbell never got hurt the way Kendric had hurt her again, but that wasn't all there was in life. She wanted more, and she wasn't going to stop until she had it. No matter the cost. "You're wrong."

Sweat dripped into her eyes, but she didn't have to see Elliot Bryon in order to take him down. Campbell rocketed her foot into the back of his knee. He went down, swinging the stoker wide. Campbell wrestled the handle from his grip. The heavy metal connected with his elbow, and an ear-piercing scream filled the open space.

Campbell shoved to her feet and ran for the door on the other side of the room. "Penny!"

"Mommy!" a familiar voice cried.

She brushed the doorknob with her uninjured hand a split second before searing pain enveloped her scalp. Elliot Bryon fisted her hair, wrenching her away from the door. Clawing at his hand, Campbell stabbed the poker backward with everything she had left. In vain.

He slammed her face into the nearest wall and the steel fell from her grip. Bone-deep aches spread along her neck and skull as Elliot spun her to face him and wrapped a grip around her throat. "Guess you can't handle getting your hands dirty, after all, Detective."

Her heart pumped too loud in her ears. A low ringing filled her head. The air in her lungs pressurized until she was sure her organs would burst. She couldn't breathe, couldn't think. She tried to pry his hand from her throat, but he was too strong. Campbell kicked at him as hard as she could. Her vision wavered. She was going to pass out.

Penny. She had to fight for Penny.

A cold burst of air exploded across her skin.

Elliot Bryon's head shot around, confusion dragging his eyebrows together.

A familiar voice stripped her nerve endings bare. "Get your damn hands off my partner."

Chapter Fourteen

"Officer Hudson, what a pleasant surprise." Elliot Bryon raised his hands in surrender, but Kendric knew better than to look a gift horse in the mouth.

Campbell slid to the floor, coughing as she tried to catch her breath.

"Mr. Bryon." Kendric took aim with his sidearm, finger over the trigger. "You're looking better than I expected for a man with two holes in his chest."

"Ah, well. Turns out my wounds weren't as severe as my surgeons thought." A hint of exhaustion and pain contorted Elliot Bryon's mouth. "Helps when you know exactly where to shoot yourself."

Campbell rolled to her side. His gut clenched as he took in the sweat, dirt and blood caked across her beautiful face. She'd fought nearly to the death for their daughter. Why the hell had it taken him so long to realize they were meant to be together? That he'd walked away from the best thing this life could ever provide?

"You okay, Bell?" he asked. "Can you walk?"

Campbell nodded, rubbing her throat as she climbed to unstable balance.

"Good. Find Penny. Get her back to the truck." Kendric raised his gaze to Elliot Bryon. "I've got this."

He didn't have to ask her twice. Campbell shuffled toward a door at the back of the building. The work of two fires chased back the numbness taking hold in his hands and feet as he kept his attention on the bastard who'd tried to destroy his world and that of Sabrina Bryon and her infant daughter. "It's over, Elliot. Sabrina told us everything."

"Are you sure about that?" Elliot asked.

Campbell almost fell through the opening she'd created at the back. The door hit the wall behind it, but she didn't go in. "Penny?"

Instinct and Elliot Bryon's casual demeanor triggered warning in Kendric's gut. "What's wrong?"

"She's not…" Campbell stumbled back, shaking her head. "She's not here. I heard her. She was calling for me. I heard her!"

"Did I forget to mention that?" Elliot Bryon

cocked his head to one side and lowered his hands.

Kendric closed the distance between him and the son of a bitch responsible for all of this. He fisted Elliot's jacket in one hand, pressing the barrel of his weapon into the man's side. Pain exploded through his shoulder, but he wasn't going to let it stop him from getting to Penny. "Where is she!"

"Tsk, tsk, tsk. That's not how you want to treat the man who holds her daughter's life in his hands, is it?" A wide smile deepened lines around the perpetrator's eyes and mouth. Then drained. "Tell you what. I'll offer you the same deal I gave to your partner there. Arrest me, and you'll never see that little girl again. Tell me where my wife is, and you have my word I'll send you Penny's location as soon as I'm clear of this backward town. I just hope you're not already too late."

"You son of a bitch. You'd let an innocent child die just to get your revenge? So you don't have to face what you've done?" Nausea churned in Kendric's gut as the answer surfaced.

Elliot shrugged as best he could. "We all have motives for making the choices we do, Officer Hudson. Mine is survival, and Sabrina is standing in my way."

"You won't get away with this, even if you do get to Sabrina," Kendric said.

"Judging from the fact you're bleeding through your shirt, I already have." Elliot nodded toward Kendric's shoulder.

Campbell moved faster than he expected. Grabbing a rifle set against one wall, she swung the butt of the weapon against Elliot Bryon's head. The man dropped harder than a sack of rocks at Kendric's feet. "That's for kidnapping my daughter."

"Well, that didn't go as expected." Admiration flooded through him. Her strength would save their daughter. He just wished he'd trusted her sooner.

"Cuff him. If Penny's not here, he wouldn't risk being out of touch to make sure she can't escape wherever he's holding her." She crouched at Elliot Bryon's side and started patting him down. Pulling a phone from the bastard's pocket, she set the device in front of the kidnapper's face to unlock the screen. "She has to be close."

Kendric collected the man's wrists behind his back and cuffed him. "There's spotty cell service out here. Even if we access it, we might not have a location."

"Then we look for her." Campbell shot to her feet, heading for the door. Muted bruises were already swelling across her face. She'd held off the suspect responsible for taking her daughter alone. Was there anything this woman couldn't do?

Kendric turned to stop her. "Campbell, you can't march out there in the middle of a blizzard to search for her. Hypothermia isn't a joke out here."

"I'm not just going to let her die, Kendric. She's my daughter," she said. "She's out there, alone and scared. All she wants is to go home, and I'll do whatever it takes to make that happen. You ran to escape the world and everyone in it. But isn't there just one person in your life you'd be willing to die for to ensure they'd live? Or are you really so angry and resentful that no one has a shot to earn your love anymore?"

His throat dried. "We have to stick together. It's the only way—"

Campbell's gaze slipped over his shoulder a split second before she swung him around. Putting her between him and the rifle in Elliot Bryon's cuffed hands.

"No!" The gunshot ripped through her back and exited her front, barely missing him. She fell forward into Kendric's chest. Her fingers fisted in his jacket but released just as quickly as she collapsed. The hard *thunk* of her knees hitting cement reverberated through him.

Elliot Bryon ran for the door and out into the storm. Gone.

Kendric's hands shook as he laid Campbell across the floor. Blood seeped between his fingers. He added pressure to the wound, but it had gone through and through. He couldn't stop the bleeding alone. "Shhh. I've got you. It's going to be okay. Just keep breathing. Okay. Try not to move."

"He's getting away." Her voice wavered as tears slipped down her cheeks. Campbell pressed her chin to her chest to get a better visual of the wound and slipped her hand over his.

"Don't worry about that. I need you to focus on staying conscious. You got me? Stay with me." After everything they'd been through, it couldn't end like this. Damn it. He needed to get her out of here. "Hang on to me. I can get you to the truck. The radios should still be working."

"You need to go," she said. "Without me. I'll just slow you down."

Not an option. Kendric fit his injured arm beneath her knees and hauled her to his chest. His strength buckled as the tendons in his shoulder threatened to dislocate. A groan clawed up his throat as he got to his feet.

"You're out of your damn mind if you think I'm leaving you."

"Penny." Campbell raised her bloodied hand to his face, following the pattern of scars on the right side. His internal shame for the physical evidence of his failure wanted him to pull away, but he couldn't. Not from her. Over the course of the past few days, she'd inexplicably become part of him. He could extricate her from his life as easily as one of his organs. He wasn't leaving her. "I thought I could protect her, but she needs you. Go. Please."

"She needs you, too. You're all she's ever known." He smoothed her hair away from her face to avoid the truth. She was right. Campbell was in no condition to brave the dropping temperatures, and any movement on her part could increase blood flow. She had to stay here. And he had to go. Kendric set her down as gently as possible. A moan escaped her control and gripped his heart in a vise. He pressed his forehead against hers. "I'll be back as soon as I can with help. Stay here. I'm not finished with you."

"I'm not finished with you, either." A weak smile exaggerated the paleness of her skin. "Bring our daughter home."

"I give you my word." Kendric slipped out the same door Elliot Bryon had escaped, leaving his heart behind. His skin contracted along the back of his neck and scalp as the storm did its job to sweep across the landscape. One arm raised to protect his face, he struggled through shin-deep snow in search of some other structure nearby, somewhere the bastard would've stashed a four-year-old. Winds whipped through the tree line that surrounded the back of the property. He hadn't spotted it on approach. Divots pockmarked pristine snow leading from the door toward those trees. If Elliot Bryon had wanted a clean escape, he'd get out of sight as quickly as possible.

Kendric jogged to catch up. There was a chance he was walking straight into a trap, but the reward at the end of this was far worth the risk. His family was all that mattered. His throat burned against freezing temperatures. He ducked into the tree line, immediately finding himself in a whole new world of muffled silence and stillness. The tracks veered northeast. No sight of Elliot Bryon or an ambush, but he couldn't discount the possibility. Tension bled down his spine as he took each step with care. The weight of being watched settled between his shoulder blades, and Kendric turned a split second before the crack of a gunshot.

The bullet whizzed by his right ear and

clipped the shell of cartilage. He pumped his legs hard, struggling through snow to get to cover. Another round ripped through the tree bark at his left.

"It's over, Officer Hudson. There's nowhere for you to go." Snow crunched beneath heavy footsteps, growing louder second by second. "That little girl is going to freeze to death because of you, and if she doesn't, she'll starve. And to think, you could've stopped any of this from happening. All you had to do was tell me where you're keeping Sabrina. You sure you can live with that choice the rest of your short life?"

Kendric pressed his skull against the tree at his back. His time had come. He could either choose to stay disconnected from the world he'd left behind—to hide from his circumstances—or he could fight his way back into it. Back to Campbell and Penny. He checked the rounds in his magazine and loaded a bullet into the chamber.

His decision was already made.

"The question isn't whether or not I can live with it, Elliot. What you should be worried about is what I'll do to find her." He brought his weapon up and took aim at the man on the other side of a small clearing.

Kendric pulled the trigger at the same time another bullet jerked Elliot Bryon's head back.

THE GUNSHOT ECHOED through the building. Louder than it should've been. Close.

For a moment, it paralyzed her lungs before only the sound of crackling flames broke through the haze. Campbell pressed her hand into the bullet wound in her side. The pain threatened to tear through her, but she'd survived heartbreak and loss and the physical pain of Penny's birth to get to this point. She wasn't going to just roll over and die. "Kendric."

The muscles in her jaw protested under the pressure of her back teeth. Another groan vibrated as she forced herself to stand. Kendric was out there against a mountain of threats. Including the damn elements themselves. If Elliot Bryon had gotten to him…

Campbell took a step forward. Then another. Her strength escaped as quickly as blood seeped from her wound, but she had to know if he'd made it. She had to know her daughter was safe. Dizziness thrust her into the doorjamb. The storm had intensified, but she'd do anything to see Penny again. To see Kendric. To sit in front of the fireplace at Whispering Pines Ranch and sleep away the day with the two of them snuggled up next to her. It wasn't a fantasy. It was as real as the cold seeping past her coat, and she wasn't going to let it slip through her fingers. "I'm coming."

Her heel caught on the stairs, and she pitched forward. Her broken hand screamed in agony as she hit the ground. Campbell rolled onto her back. Snow melted against her face as the world threatened darkness and hollowness and cold. She had to get up. Gravity tried to convince her this was where she needed to be. Right here in the open, beneath a cloud-covered sky with the trees and mountains to protect her, but her heart warned otherwise. It infused her with an energy she hadn't known existed and allowed her to get off the ground.

The wind burned against her skin and whipped her hair into her face. Pinpricks of numbness climbed up her fingers as she pushed toward the trees. The blood leaking from the bullet wound had slowed with the frigid temperatures. Or her body had already started shutting down. She wasn't sure which one she preferred. Either way, she wasn't going to stop until she found Penny and Kendric. Her throat tightened as she hummed the lullaby she sang to her daughter every night before bed. "Twinkle, twinkle, I love you."

Silence descended all around her as the storm failed to batter against the surrounding trees. Two sets of tracks led northeast of her position, but every cell in her body had her following a different path. She shuffled through heavy snow, her jaw no longer quivering to keep her warm. She'd stopped shivering altogether. "Ooh, my baby, this is true."

"When you snuggle next to me," a small voice said. "I'm as happy as can be."

Campbell froze. She'd already lost too much blood, but she hadn't imagined it. Spinning in circles, she searched the whitewashed wilderness for signs of life. She caught sight of a small shed tucked back, camouflaged in snow and wood. She took a step forward. This was it. It had to be. Because if she was hallucinating... Her stomach revolted against the idea. "Penny?"

"Mommy!" The solid wood door of the shed—brand-new from the look of it—jerked against an equally solid padlock with a combination dial.

"Penny! Hold on. I'm coming, baby." The snow was deeper here. It fell into the tops of her boots and soaked her jeans straight through. Campbell pulled on the padlock with everything she had, but it wouldn't budge. Elliot Bryon had taken her gun, she'd left the hammer in the abandoned smithing building and there was no chance in hell she'd guess the combination to the lock. She swept bloody hands down the door. "I'm going to get you out of there. I promise."

"Mommy, I want you. I want to go home," Penny said. "The man took me from Grandma and Papa. I tried to scream, but he wouldn't let me. He said I had to be quiet or he'd hurt them. I'm sorry, Mommy. I just want to go home."

"I know. I know. It's not your fault. We're going to go home. Okay? I'm right here. I just need to find something to break the lock." Pain flared into her side, and Campbell doubled over. Catching herself on a fallen tree, she forced herself to catch her breath.

"Don't leave me! Mommy!" Anxiety punctuated the girl's kicks against the shed door.

"I'm...right here, baby." Her vision distorted as she pulled her hand free of her wound. The faster her heart beat, the faster she'd bleed out. The trees tilted on their axis despite the added leverage of her hand on one of the wood's fallen soldiers. It was harder to breathe now. Heavier on her chest. "I'm not going anywhere."

Campbell pulled at the branch in her hand. Desperation flooded through her as she tried again and again. But it wouldn't break.

"Mommy!" Penny's cries pierced through the low ringing in her ears. "I want out of here!"

"I'm here. I'm not leaving you, Penny. I'm…" The world ripped out from under her. Ice infiltrated the collar of her coat as she tried to find that legendary strength she'd always relied on. Why couldn't she use it when she needed it the most? Being run off the road, surviving a rollover, resisting a drug and an interrogation, getting through heartbreak and isolation and loneliness not once but twice, the trauma of Penny's birth and hearing the love of her life had been caught in a deadly explosion—none of that had broken her.

This wouldn't, either.

Campbell hauled her hand up, and she latched onto the same branch she'd tried to dislocate to get back on her feet. Wood groaned in her hand until it gave way, and she stumbled back. A small sense of victory charged through her, but this was only the beginning. She still had to break the lock. The oversize branch dragged behind her as she trod through another pass of snow. "Get back, baby. I don't want you to get hurt."

Bringing her makeshift bat over her shoulder, she bit back the scream of pain and put everything she had into swinging it as hard as she could. The padlock bounced, then settled back into place. She swung again, angling down to separate the lock from the mechanism. Twice. Three times.

The padlock busted along one side. Relief softened the tension in her legs, and she fell forward against the door. Wrenching it open, she reached for the four-year-old lunging at her from the dark. Mangled, matted hair caught in her fingers as she clutched Penny to her chest. "It's okay now. I'm here. You're safe."

A glimmer of light in one corner of the shed stared down at them. The light from a small camera. The bastard had been surveilling Penny the entire time. Had most likely put a similar camera in the smithy building. That was how she'd been able to hear Penny's cries. Elliot Bryon had set out to not only physically punish her but emotionally and mentally destroy her. But it hadn't worked. Campbell framed her daughter's small face between both hands and kissed her cheek. "Let's get out of here. Okay?"

Penny nodded, her tear-streaked face coated with dirt.

Campbell picked up her daughter and retraced her steps through the trees. Managing the added weight kicked up her heart rate. She just had to get Penny to the truck. From there they could call for backup if Kendric hadn't already.

They left the safety of the trees, every sense she owned on alert for something off. The crush of wind and snow stole her breath. She tucked her coat around Penny and held on tight. Her exhalations weren't fogging in front of her mouth anymore. Her body temperature had dropped too far.

They weren't going to make it.

Tears froze on her cheeks as snow caught in her lashes. Mere minutes would separate them from life and death out here. Campbell smoothed her daughter's hair against her head and tucked deeper against Penny's cold ear. Her side had soaked through with blood. "I love you. You know that, right? You know I'll always protect you. No matter what. You were the best thing that ever happened in my life. Do you understand? I don't regret a single moment we had together. I love you so much."

"I love you, too, Mommy." Penny pressed her pink face into Campbell's neck, squishing her arms between them.

Her strength gave out. Campbell's knees buckled, and she wrapped her arms around Penny's back to soften the coming blow. They fell in a tangle of limbs into a cushion of snow, her daughter trapped beneath her. She couldn't force her body to respond.

"Mommy, get up! You have to get up.

I'm stuck." Penny's scream pierced through the dizziness determined to pull her under. "Mommy, a man!"

"It's okay, Penny. I'm a friend of your mom's. I'm not going to hurt you. I'm here to help. Okay? Your mom's going to be okay. I promise. I'll get you someplace warm." A dark outline took shape beside them. So familiar. Safe. Warmth encased her back as the shape pressed a large hand between her shoulder blades. "Damn it, woman. I told you to stay put."

Her desperation to keep Penny close fired as he pulled her daughter free. Campbell reached to hang on to her even as recognition soothed her fight-or-flight instincts. "No."

"I've got her, Bell." Kendric soothed Penny's back as the four-year-old's sobs intensified. "Over here!" He turned back to her, his hand still in place. "Stay with us, Campbell. Don't you dare give up. We need you. Penny and I need you."

A myriad of voices filtered in and out as lethargy and cold and pain took hold. She didn't know if she could do as he asked. Going to sleep felt like a much better solution.

"Here, I'll hold Penny. You and Isla take care of Campbell," a male voice said. The chief?

Another rush of movement penetrated her

vision. Although she couldn't pick out one distinct shape from another, she had the feeling she was being moved. She wasn't cold anymore. Campbell gave in to the weight of her eyelids as exhaustion sucked her down.

"Vitals are slowing." Another voice weaved through the darkness. "I'm losing her!"

Chapter Fifteen

"Open your eyes, Campbell." Kendric squeezed her hand again, but it was no use. The surgeon who'd stitched up her insides from Elliot Bryon's bullet had advised him her recovery would take time. Days. Maybe weeks. Not good enough. He needed her to look at him, to ensure him everything was going to be okay.

Was this how she'd felt at the side of his hospital bed after that bomb had torn his life apart? The impatience. The worry. The second-guessing. How had she survived?

Monitors chimed consistent rhythms from the other side of the bed. Bruising and lacerations flawed the creamy skin of her arms and face, but she'd regained more color since her surgery two days ago. Kendric sandwiched her hand between both of his and kissed her torn knuckles. She'd fought like hell to get Penny back, putting her life in danger not once but twice. He'd never forget her strength, her love and commitment.

"Any change?" Isla Vach slipped into the room as quiet as a ghost, almost ambushing him. Or had his defenses worn out since leaving those woods?

"Nothing yet." He counted off the pulse at the base of Campbell's neck.

The EMT rounded into his peripheral vision. "She's been through a lot. Lost a lot of blood. Not to mention exposure to freezing temperatures. It might take some—"

"Time. Yeah. So I've been told." Pressing his cheek to Campbell's hand, he fought the exhaustion slithering through his veins. The past forty-eight hours had undermined every choice he'd made since leaving Denver, but he knew exactly where he wanted to be from now on. Right here. With Campbell. Forever. "How's Penny doing?"

"Good. She and Mazi are having a blast together at the ranch. I think Chief Ford is going to try to help them build snow forts this afternoon. She asks about her mom when she slows down enough to think, which isn't often, I'll admit, but she's getting through it. Especially with Karie Ford's baked goods." Isla took an empty seat on the opposite side of the bed. "How are you?"

"I'm fine." He wasn't sure how many "I'm fines" that made. He'd lost count within the first couple of hours of waiting for Campbell to come out of surgery, but he appreciated the concern. From Isla. From Easton Ford and Genevieve. Even Gregson and Alma had made it a point to check in on him. "Any news I might've missed?"

"Chief Ford closed the case against Sabrina Bryon. From what that district attorney said, she'll most likely get time served because of her circumstances with a new baby. She did abduct and kidnap a law enforcement officer, so she doesn't get off scot-free, but your chief thought it better to let her move on with her life. Unfortunately, we'll never know what kind of life that'll be. Seems she took off after your department got your and Campbell's location. Nobody has seen her or the baby since." Isla got to her feet, studying the monitors recording Campbell's vitals.

His gut said they wouldn't. "What happened with the Jane Doe we found? Rachel Stephenson."

"Now, that's an interesting story. Turns out Sabrina wrestled Rachel's gun away during the struggle at the cabin. It's the gun she used to shoot you." Isla backed away from the monitors. "The crime lab connected the bullet in your shoulder to six other unsolved murder investigations along the West Coast. Seems Rachel Stephenson was exactly who Sabrina Bryon claimed. A hired killer working at her husband's beck and call as long as he was connected to her bosses down south. Now that the investigation is closed, I imagine her body will be returned to her family, if she has any. In my experience, people in her line of work don't have many personal connections. They can't afford to."

"What experience is that?" he asked.

A weak smile thinned the EMT's mouth as she took her seat again. "Have you figured out who shot Elliot Bryon yet?"

"No." Kendric still couldn't get the image of the man's head snapping back with the bullet between his eyes. A shot like that wasn't easy, but nobody in BMPD had come forward to take credit. Dr. Chloe Pascale had sent the bullet to the crime lab in Denver, but it would be weeks before they heard anything. "I keep replaying what happened, but nothing jumps out. Whoever took the shot is one hell of a marksman. They managed to stay out of sight, hit their target and get out of there without being seen."

Almost like Sabrina Bryon had from the primary crime scene.

"I'm sure you and your fellow boys in blue will find the shooter. Which reminds me, they've recovered Elliot Bryon's handgun, the one he used to shoot himself. I don't know how he pulled it off, but he hid it in a secret compartment under his side of his and Sabrina's bed. Right where EMTs found him after the 911 call. His prints were the only ones left behind. Same goes for the boots that went with him to the hospital. A nurse found him trying to toss them in one of the hazardous waste bins. Guess he knew you and Detective Dwyer were closing in," she said. "Listen, Hudson, I know I'm just an EMT and not exactly part of your department, but I can take a shift to sit with her if you want to get some sleep or head down to the cafeteria."

"I'd prefer to stay with her. Thanks, though. For everything." He turned back to Campbell. "If it weren't for you, she might not have made it."

"Anytime." Isla pushed to her feet, heading for the door. "You've got my number in case you need to get a hold of me. I'm happy to watch Penny as long as you need."

The door closed behind her as though she'd never visited.

"You should've let her stay. You look like hell." Campbell's hand twitched in his, and he caught the barest glimpse of her cerulean eyes beneath heavy lids staring across the bed at him.

Kendric sat forward in his seat, his heart shooting straight into his throat. Relief unlike anything he'd felt before produced a burn in his eyes, and he clutched her hand against his chest. "Hey. Welcome back to the land of the living, Detective. How do you feel?"

"Like you should remember I'm not a detective." Her lips curled at one corner of her mouth. She took in the room around her, the IV feeding into her vein, him. "Where's Penny?"

"At the ranch. Chief Ford and Chloe are watching her until you're recovered enough. I wasn't sure having her here was the best idea." He soothed pressure into the space between her thumb and index finger. "She's been asking for you. She wants to make sure you're okay."

"And my parents?" she asked.

"They're here, and they're fine," he said. "Elliot Bryon didn't hurt them. They've been apologizing and agonizing since the moment they got to town, but they're happy Penny and you are safe."

"Good. The last thing I remember is getting her out of that shed." Campbell moved to lift one arm, stopped by the IV in her arm. She tugged her hand free of his and set it against the wound in her side. "What happened out there?"

"Not much. I followed Elliot Bryon's tracks into the woods, hoping he'd gone for wherever he was keeping Penny. It was an ambush. He fired a couple rounds, but in the end, he was the one to take a bullet." Kendric fit a strand of her matted hair away from her face. "You and Penny don't have to worry about him anymore."

"That's good news." She settled back against the pillows, her expression softening. "You came for me. Even after we said all those things to each other."

"Yeah. Not my proudest moment." He collected the shattered snow globe from where he'd set it on the table beside her bed and handed it over. "I found this in the SUV. I'm sorry to say it didn't survive my driving skills, but I recognized it from the first Christmas we were together. I didn't realize you'd kept it all this time."

"This is why you risked your life for me and Penny?" she asked.

"As much as I wanted to keep living in my misery, I knew if I was wrong about you, it wouldn't matter if I made it out of there alive." Regret and a million other emotions collected at the base of his skull. "I'm sorry, Bell. For leaving you all those years ago. For not being there to help raise Penny. For thinking you were using me to investigate my department. I have no excuse. I was wrong, and angry and feeling like a failure in every aspect of my life. That's why I ran to the ATF, why I resigned after Agent Freehan tried to destroy this town. I thought if I could fix what was broken, I could be someone worthy of you and your love. That I would finally be good enough for you again. And when I failed at even that, I took it out on you and your job with Internal Affairs, but you're the one who deserves better than someone like me. I want to do better. I want to prove I can be the man you and Penny believe I am."

She turned the broken snow globe in her hand before offering it back. "I kinda like the you you've become."

"Just kind of?" A smile pulled at his mouth. "Is that all?"

"Well, I mean, there's room for improvement. For both of us. But yeah." She nodded. "I remember lying facedown in the snow, and I heard your voice. You kept telling me to hang on while you were holding Penny."

The image crystallized so clearly in his mind, forcing him to relive the worst moment of his life all over again. His throat dried, and he wanted nothing more than to hold her, to make sure this was real.

"You were trying to calm her down while you kept one hand on my back." She motioned over her shoulder with her free hand before returning her gaze to his. "That's what I want, Kendric. I watched you detach from your family and friends, your coworkers, me. I saw how the bombing stripped more than a few layers of skin from your face, and there was nothing I could do to hold on to you. But seeing you with Penny, trying to comfort her despite the fact I was losing consciousness—it showed me how much we've been missing. There isn't a single thing you have to prove to me or anyone else. You can be angry, you can change jobs or move to another town if you have to, you can run. Move to Denver or don't. It doesn't matter. We just need you to love us. Do you think you can manage that, Officer Hudson?"

Kendric traced his thumb along the back of her hand, memorizing the pattern of veins beneath the thin skin. He'd imagined this moment so many times, the invitation to come home and be part of Campbell's life again, the weight of his isolation and anger a distant memory. He'd scripted answers a thousand times, but right now, none of them came to mind. Because this wasn't a fantasy. She was real. Penny was real, and he wasn't going to take a single moment of his future with them for granted. He kissed her hand, aggravating his own wound in his shoulder. Just proof this wasn't all in his head. "Yeah, Detective Dwyer. I think I can manage that."

"DON'T PUT THAT in your mouth!" Kendric lunged across the kitchen. "No, that doesn't mean you can lick it off the floor, either. There's no five-second rule for juice and places we put our feet."

A high-pitched laugh trilled through the living room as Penny ran down the hallway into her new bedroom. Campbell couldn't help but laugh at the absurdity of their life at the moment. The move from Denver hadn't been easy as she was still recovering from the wound in her side, but Kendric had ordered the movers around like no one's business. The renovated farmhouse they'd found just outside Battle Mountain was perfect. High ceilings, tall enough for the massive fir tree Weston and Easton Ford had dragged inside, lit up with the addition of white Christmas lights and silvery ornaments. The four-foot-deep island in the kitchen allowed all three of them to bake cookies as many times as they wanted with plenty of room left over. And the enlarged soaker tub in the main bathroom had held its own more than enough times since they'd moved in. Absolutely perfect. But none of it meant a damn without the two most important people in the world.

The sectional cushions dipped as Kendric collapsed beside her, winded. Tugging her legs onto his lap, he fanned heated hands across her shins. "I don't understand it. We kicked the soccer ball around for an hour. I took her to the park. She hasn't had any sugar today other than the juice she just tried to lick off the floor. It's like she runs on never-ending batteries. Does she ever get tired?"

"No, but she sleeps through everything." Campbell set the book she'd been reading aside, pulled his head closer and planted a kiss at his temple. The past few weeks had been everything she'd dreamed. Her CO had accepted her resignation with understanding, albeit disappointment. Officers willing to dive into the Internal Affairs world came along few and far between, but they'd manage without her. She'd miss it. Investigating. Helping people, but until the bullet wound in her side had healed completely, she was out of the game. Not a total loss. Watching Kendric try to parent a stubborn and energetic four-year-old girl had its perks.

"Everything, huh? I like the sound of that." He scratched at his ear, refusing to look at her, but she knew him well enough to follow his line of thought. "What did the doctor say at your three-week follow-up?"

She nudged him with the spine of her book. "Looks good. Minimal scarring considering Isla's fine work to stitch me back together. The woman does good work."

"Anything else?" His voice notched a bit higher as though his nerves had gotten the better of him. "Extracurricular activities you've been cleared for?"

"Such as?" She liked this game. Forcing him to talk about what he wanted—sometimes what he needed—instead of bottling it up to explode later. It was a habit they both had to explore, but the trust was there now. Something they hadn't really had before the explosion all those years ago. Not like this. With Penny to care for, they didn't have any other choice, and Campbell liked it that way. No more secrets. No more half-truths or distance. They were in this together. Partners. Forever.

"Oh, I don't know. Making out and stuff. Just off the top of my head," he said.

"We do that now." She couldn't keep her smile to herself. Their makeup sessions had been fun the past few weeks. Nothing like two bullet wounds to make a woman appreciate the sensuality she'd been missing since nearly losing the father of her child to a madman.

Offense contorted his expression. "We don't do stuff."

"Oh, it's the stuff you're interested in. I see. I misunderstood." Campbell leaned forward, slower than she wanted to go, and pressed her mouth to his ear. "Here I thought you were complaining about my kissing skills."

A scoff escaped his control. The perfect compliment to the red flaring in his cheeks. A shiver chased across his shoulders as she nibbled on the shell of his ear. "No complaints here."

"That's what I thought." She settled back against the arm of the couch and cracked the spine of her book.

"You're not going to tell me, are you?" Kendric set his head back against the sofa. The too-tense, isolated and disconnected reserve officer she'd met at that primary crime scene didn't exist anymore. Not with her, at least. In his place sat the very human, inspiring and hopeful man she'd fallen in love with all over again. A man she wanted to raise her daughter with, one she envisioned growing old with her here in Battle Mountain. This place was home now. Because of him.

"Tell you what?" She dropped her book slightly, enough to give her a view of the desperation in his gaze. "Oh, we're still talking about this? For your information, the doctor did have something to say about stuff at my appointment today. He said he will get back to me."

"You're killing me," he said.

"I'm teasing. He said we're all clear, and I can't wait to show you exactly what you walked away from five years ago." She lifted her eyebrows suggestively.

"A mistake I regret every single day." A low moan strained in his throat. "You're going to drive me insane."

"Just wait. It gets better. Just as soon as Penny goes to bed for the night." Campbell delighted in her ability to set him off with a single look, a single touch. The man beneath her resembled a ticking time bomb. One wrong move, and she'd find herself in his control. "I'm telling you. Nothing wakes that girl once she's asleep. Then you can have me all to yourself."

"Okay. That's great news. We just have to wait until then." Kendric tapped his fingers in an even rhythm against her shin. "Until then you can tell me the truth about why you joined Internal Affairs."

"It doesn't really matter, does it?" she asked. "I turned in my resignation."

He poked her shoulder. "While I was in the hospital for burn treatment, two officers in suits came in to ask me about what happened. They wouldn't tell me who they were or which precinct they were from, so I didn't give them anything. Told them to read my statement." He didn't wait for her response. "They came to you, didn't they? They threatened to open an investigation into me unless you cooperated, and when I left you to raise a baby on your own, they leveraged your career against you. Got you to work for them."

"I wasn't going to let them ruin your reputation or charge you for something that wasn't your fault." She closed her book. "Not after everything you'd been through."

"Why didn't you tell me sooner?" he asked.

"Would you have believed me? Would you have listened to me after the words *Internal Affairs*?" The answer was already in his expression, but none of that mattered now. "Like I said, it doesn't matter now. I'm happy right where I am. With you and Penny, here." She pressed her mouth to his. "Any sign of Sabrina Bryon?"

"Not yet. She's good at disappearing, and now that she's got justice for her sister's death, I don't think we'll see her anytime soon," he said.

"You still think she's the one who shot Elliot Bryon in those woods—Dean Pratt—whoever he was?" she asked.

"Makes the most sense. He tried to kill her and their unborn baby. Stands to reason she'd want to make sure he couldn't come after her again. Although, we'll never have the proof, and it was in defense of a Battle Mountain reserve officer. No prosecutor will come within ten feet of bringing charges." Kendric wedged his uninjured hand against his head, that forest green gaze warming in an instant. "What time does Penny go to bed again?"

"Four more hours." She got back to pretending to read her book, pretending as though his insinuations didn't have an effect on her at all. Between figuring out their new relationship, caring for two bullet wounds, moving in together, resigning from her job and ensuring Penny could accept the new addition to their family, their physical relationship had been limited to a G rating. But with him staring at her as though she were the only woman in the world... She couldn't think of anything else but testing that rating. "Nothing you can't handle, right?"

The crash of something significant and heavy ripped them from the bubble they'd created around themselves. Kendric hauled her legs off him long enough to escape and get to his feet. "I had more luck with the bomb that blew off the right side of my face."

"And yet, you're still as handsome as ever." She watched him disappear down the hallway.

"Holy—" Silence descended for a series of breaths. "Penny Elana Dwyer, you were gone for two minutes. How on earth did you manage… You know what? No. I give up." Heavy footsteps registered. "Bell, she's going to need a bath. And so is the rest of her room. Do you think the fire department would let us borrow one of their hoses?"

The joys of parenthood. Campbell plugged her nose as she identified the problem without moving from her spot on the couch. And the smells. Vapor rub. An entire room smeared with vapor rub. "No. They stopped answering our calls when you called the paramedics after she scraped her knee outside."

"That thing took forever to stop bleeding. I thought she was potassium deficient." Kendric opened the front door, then the back and all the windows in the main living area.

"I'll get her in the bath. You clean up whatever she used to paint her room." Campbell had enough experience to know exactly how long it would take to clean vapor rub off the walls and her daughter's toys. Some of them still had a film from last year. Her side twinged as she got to her feet, but she wasn't going to let this wound stop her from living her life. Or enjoying having Kendric back.

Suspicion narrowed his gaze as he turned on her. "How do you know she painted her room? Has she done this before? Is it going to happen again?"

"Welcome to parenting, honey." She kissed him lightly on the lips, throwing a parody of his first words to her after she'd come to Battle Mountain back at him. "You're going to love it."

Campbell headed down the hallway, grateful this wasn't a job she had to do on her own anymore, and that Penny would be able to breathe clearly for the next few days.

He called after her. "You never answered my question. Is this going to keep happening?"

Campbell started the tub. "I think you already know the answer to that."

Epilogue

Isla Vach stripped gloves from her hands and tossed them into the garbage.

Her twelve-hour shift was officially over. Everyone was saved. She could finally pick up Mazi from Whispering Pines Ranch for their annual Christmas movie marathon tonight.

Collecting her purse from her locker, she smiled at the sound of jokes and laughter of the firefighters upstairs at dinner. Battle Mountain Fire and Rescue had run off volunteers for years, but after the forest fire a few months back, the state had provided funds to hire a full EMT staff and pay the men and women who'd run headfirst into the flames. Just her luck, too. Going back to work hadn't ever been part of her and Clint's plan after they'd had Mazi.

But things had changed on his last deployment.

Now it was up to her to be there for their daughter. Flaws and all.

"Movie marathon night, right?" one of the firefighters asked.

"Yeah. Just leaving." She pulled her keys from her purse. "It's going to be a rager until about eight o'clock when Mazi passes out."

"Have a great night, Isla." He moved toward the stairs, most likely angling to get his share of dinner before it was gone. "Say hello to Mazi for me, will you?"

"Will do. Good night." Crisp December air closed around her as she walked through the engine bay toward her car across the street. It had been a mostly quiet night. Two calls. Nothing she and her partner hadn't been able to handle. Nothing like the terror she'd faced trying to stitch up Kendric and Campbell a few weeks ago. She could live without that kind of anxiety again.

Isla lined her key between her index and middle finger and approached her car. Her reflection warbled in the frosted glass. She used the sleeve of her coat to dislodge some of it, catching sight of movement behind her.

A hard wall of muscle slammed her into the ground a split second before a gunshot ripped through her.

* * * * *

COUNTRY LEGACY COLLECTION

19 FREE BOOKS IN ALL!

Cowboys, adventure and romance await you in this new collection! Enjoy superb reading all year long with books by bestselling authors like **Diana Palmer, Sasha Summers and Marie Ferrarella!**